Mardi Gras

a Toni & Bart time-travel tale

Mardi Gras

a Toni & Bart time-travel tale
Diane Wordsworth
This novella has been published in *Words Worth Reading*

Baggins Bottom Books

Also by Diane Wordsworth

Marcie Craig mysteries
Night Crawler

Tarot Tales
The Ace of Wands
The Ace of Cups

Toni & Bart time-travel tales
Mardi Gras

Wordsworth Collections
Twee Tales
Twee Tales Too
Twee Tales Twee
Flash Fiction: Five Very Short Stories

Words Worth Reading

Issue 1: October 2021

Wordsworth Shorts
The Spirit of the Wind
The Most Scariest Night of the Year
The Girl on the Bench
Dancing on Ice
Happy Christmas, Santa
Careful What You Wish For
New Year's Revolution
One Born Every Minute
The Mystery of Woolley Dam
Martha's Favourite Doll
The Complete Angler
Alexandra's Ragtag Band

Wordsworth Writers' Guides
Diary of a Scaredy Cat
Project Management for Writers: Gate 1 – What?

Watch for more at https://dianewordsworth.com.

for Ian, always

Chapter 1

THE EDDY PICKED UP speed as it sucked them both down and into its depths. Down, down, down, until they couldn't breathe properly, until they thought they'd never breathe again. At that precise moment there was a bump, restarting the supply of oxygen, and Bart stopped clawing at his throat. He knew it would be all right, but it still threw him into a panic.

He felt Toni's hand reach out for his. His sister knew, she always knew how it got him, and while she couldn't speak, while they couldn't yet communicate, and while they couldn't properly see each other, this was always how she gave him courage. Just by reaching out a hand and touching his.

He felt another bump as the colours changed from white silver to white gold, to yellow, to orange. The specks of dust would turn into little stars next, then big stars, then the planets, as they reached their programmed destination. Only the specks didn't turn into little stars this time. This time there was an extra bump – that wasn't supposed to be there, he thought – then a bit of a rumble. And the orange light changed to red and then deep vermilion.

As it span faster and faster, he realised there was something wrong. No, no, no, no, no. This wasn't supposed to happen. This never happened. It was going too fast.

He reached out his other hand to find Toni's. Her fingers were cold. She wasn't expecting this either and her fingers squeezed his more tightly than ever. This wasn't her reassuring grip. This was a "what's happening?" grip. And until they actually stopped, if they ever stopped, they wouldn't be able to speak. But at least he could see her eyes come into focus, staring out through the opening in her helmet.

Well, if it was going to go wrong, at least they were together. They always had that to booster their confidence, like a little joke about a circumstance that would never, ever happen. It was never supposed to happen.

Bart squeezed Toni's hands and pulled her a little closer to him as the darkness closed in around them.

His nostrils twitched as the vortex bumped and skittered again. Burning. Something was burning. He looked around him wildly, and he saw Toni do the same. The dark redness was turning smoky. Something was on fire. The machine was on fire. And it was slowing down. It was coming in to land – crash-land more like.

Bart was finally able to pull Toni into a hug, and they clung on to each other. He pulled his legs up so he was in a foetal position, and she mimicked him. He remembered someone telling them once to keep their arms and legs in. "Curl up, don't put your hands out. You'll hurt yourself if you put your hands out."

As the machine finally came to land, the g-force propelling it and them forward, they clung together and rolled with it.

Bart felt the first bounce, then the second, and then three more before they finally crashed against something that sent shockwaves through his entire body. Toni yelped out an involuntary scream, which meant their time had come, they'd arrived at their destination, or at least a destination of sorts.

And then all went quiet and still and black.

AS THE MACHINE CRASHED against a moss-covered boulder, sparks shot everywhere and two people fell out of an opening that wasn't even there before. Originally entwined, they came apart, tumbled along the ground, and landed in an eventual heap, both knocked out by the fall.

The smell of blood oozing from their fresh wounds and into the dirt alerted a local resident snake. Initially alarmed and then curious, it started to slither towards them.

Chapter 2

THE HELMET HAD FALLEN off her head before she landed and rolled a few feet away. Toni's head hurt and every bone in her body felt as though she'd been trampled by a herd of elephants.

She heard a groan, thought it was Bart, and realised it was her. She mentally checked herself over, making sure there were no broken bones, and she opened her eyes to the weak sunlight, her vision blurred but already was starting to clear.

Toni carefully pulled herself up into a slightly sitting, slightly lying position and moved her head slowly to see where they were. It looked like the Everglades, which meant they weren't too far off the mark. She rubbed a sore part of her elbow and cast around to see if she could see Bart.

She found him only a few feet away, he too in the process of checking his injuries. He sat up slowly and removed his helmet.

Her head itched. She lifted her hand to scratch it but instead felt a warm wetness. Pulling her hand away she saw it covered with blood. And then the sore part on her head suddenly kicked in. Ouch, it stung! There was blood running down Bart's face too.

"Are you all right?" she asked, getting onto her hands and knees.

"I think so," he replied. "You don't look so great."

"Gee, thanks," she laughed.

Well, she still had her sense of humour. She wasn't dead yet.

Bart got up a bit more quickly than she did and she saw the dizziness embrace him.

"You have blood on your face," she said, gradually climbing to a standing position herself.

"You have blood all over your head," he said, coming towards her. He stooped to pick up her helmet. "What have I told you about fastening your chinstrap properly?" he said, waving the helmet at her. She was about to retort with a smart reply when he stumbled over a root and collapsed to the floor again. And then he froze.

"What's wrong? Did you hurt something else?" she asked.

"Ssh!" She started to move towards him. "Stay there," he hissed.

Toni froze too. In slow motion Bart reached out for a heavy branch, discarded it as it was still joined to a tree root, and scrabbled as quietly as he could for a rock instead. Then he hurled the rock at Toni, frightening her half to death.

Impulsively, she ducked away from the flying missile, but it totally missed her and landed in a squelch behind her. She turned to look and saw a snake with its head stoved-in by the stone.

"I thought you were throwing that at me!" she shouted, relief making her bad-tempered.

He shrugged as if to say, well, you can see that I didn't. And he climbed to his feet once again, this time more slowly.

"I wonder where we are," he said, glancing around at their surroundings. He handed Toni her helmet. "That wound looks like it needs a stitch."

She took the helmet sheepishly, dug into the pocket of her skirt to find an old dried-up tissue and pressed that in a wad against her head. "This will have to do until we find some help." And she held it there knowing her arm would start to ache soon.

"Where are we?" Bart wondered again, looking about them again. "It *looks* like the Everglades. So at least we're in the right country... unless they have Everglade-type environments all over the place."

"If it *is* the Everglades, there will be more to worry about than that," she replied, nodding towards the dead snake.

"Something went wrong," he said.

"I thought so too."

"And did you smell that fire towards the end?" She nodded. "I reckon something burnt out."

"It smelt like hydraulic fluid to me," she said, wrinkling her nose at the thought. "I remember the clutch went once on my dad's car. The hydraulic fluid got too hot and the slave cylinder caught fire. All the hydraulics went and I could smell that smell on everything for days afterwards. It really sticks in your nose."

They looked sadly towards the machine. "It'll need repairing," said Bart. "But first, we need to get you to a doctor."

"Oh, I'm all right–"

"You're not. That tissue's soaked right through. What are you going to use next?"

They took their helmets back to the machine and stowed them in the side-car. Toni picked up her classy top hat and gave it a dust. But she was too sore to place it on top of her curly head.

"Come on then, let's start walking," she said.

FORTUNATELY IT WASN'T raining, but the atmosphere was quite humid. Toni could feel her curls frizzing. Bart's hair was curly too, but he kept it too short for it to be a problem.

"This won't be good for the machine," mused Bart. "If there's a break in any of the circuits, or even in any of the wiring, this damp will cause it to misfire."

"I don't think crash-landing in the Everglades will do it a world of good either," replied Toni.

"If that's where we are..."

"Wherever we are, it still won't have been any good."

The marshy, root-ridden ground was tough to negotiate in her low-heeled ankle boots, but she managed. It didn't take them long to reach the road, even if it was just a dirt-packed shrub-lined track.

"Which way do you think we should go?" asked Bart, looking left. "I can't see anything for miles this way."

Toni looked to the right. She thought it was more built-up in the distance. But there didn't seem to be a lot of life and there were certainly no road vehicles. "That way looks like something," she said. "It doesn't look far."

As they drew nearer to the small town, they saw a road sign:

WELCOME TO NEW ORLEANS

"Well, that's handy," grinned Bart.

"It's where we were headed," agreed Toni.

"It doesn't look very... " he cast around for the right words "... modern."

"We *were* going back in time," said Toni. "*And* we were supposed to land quite close to where we would probably find the artefact we've been sent for."

"Hmm, yes," agreed Bart. "So either we landed in the wrong place..."

"Or we landed in the right place, wrong time...?"

"Exactly."

"If we're in New Orleans, then this isn't the Everglades," said Toni.

"It must be the Mississippi Delta," replied her brother.

"Mm. The ocean won't be far away." She sniffed, but she couldn't smell any sea air.

"And nor will the city," said Bart. "Come on, this isn't getting you to a doctor."

"Won't we have to pay?"

"We have money, remember."

"Yes, but if we've gone too far, it might not have been printed yet..."

So many things were whirling around inside Toni's head. Perhaps it was the bump. Perhaps she was concussed.

"It's because we've landed in the wrong place," she tried to reassure herself.

"What?" said Bart.

"Sorry. Talking to myself."

"Hmm. Come on. Doctor."

They followed the packed dirt track until the town in the distance turned into a small city closer up, and soon they were wandering the back streets looking for a doctor. Their clothes and probably their hairstyles attracted a few curious looks, but that could also be the blood. A cheerful lady wearing a red dress and a matching head scarf and carrying a heavy basket of brightly coloured fruit on her head stopped to ask if they were all right.

"My sister needs a doctor," said Bart.

"What happened to you?" asked the lady. The beads around her neck and dangling from her ears rattled as she spoke.

"We were in an accident," said Toni.

"It looks like it," said the lady. "Down the next road on the right, third door along, someone there will help."

"How much will that cost?" asked Toni.

The lady looked them up and down and reached up inside her basket. "Give him these mangoes, tell him Veronique sent you. He won't charge you then."

"Oh, but we want to pay—"

"He'll be offended if you offer. He'll appreciate the fruit."

"Who should we ask for?" asked Bart, taking the mangoes from her.

The lady chuckled, a deep-throated chortle. "There's only he there, child. But his name's Desmond."

"Thank you very much. You're very helpful."

"It's Mardi Gras week," replied Veronique. "Peaceful happy time to all." And off she waddled, basket of fruit perched securely on her head.

Chapter 3

THEY FOUND THE DOORWAY easily enough. It was the one painted in several different bright colours.

"Now if she'd told us that," laughed Bart.

There was no knocker, just a giant handle. He knocked on the door... and a witch-doctor opened it. Toni sprang backwards with surprise. The bones on the man's head rattled as he looked from one to the other.

"Ha ha ha," he boomed, making the orange, red and yellow feathers around his head shake and tremble. Removing the headdress, he said, "It's Mardi Gras. I was just trying it on for size."

"We're, er, looking for Desmond," said Bart, cautiously.

"And you have found he," said the witch-doctor.

Bart told him their names. "Veronique asked us to give you these." He held out the fruit, which Desmond took with a big smile, filled with sparkling white as well as missing teeth.

"Come in, come in. I can see why Veronique sent you." He opened the door wide with one hand and gestured towards the blood on their clothes with the other. "We'll make you some coffee, fix your wounds, and find you something to wear while we wash those..." He hesitated as he saw what they were wearing. Then he nodded his approval. "I like. Very much."

The house, or shop, or whatever it was, was like a cave filled with all sorts of interesting and colourful things hanging from the ceilings and piled on every surface. Some were quite ordinary knick-knacks, others were voodoo-related or religious.

Toni and Bart dipped so that their heads didn't bump into feathers, shrunken heads, bone necklaces, various talismans on various lengths of leather thong, crystals, amulets, things made from glass, rag dolls, wax effigies and candles. And they emerged into a lounge area furnished with stuffed chairs and over-sized floor cushions, beads and tassels hanging everywhere, but shiny surfaces reflecting light in various jewel colours. It certainly wasn't dark and dowdy. It was actually quite a fun, cheerful place.

"You're very kind," said Toni, sinking with relief into one of the over-stuffed chairs.

In an adjoining room a child, aged about twelve or thirteen, busied herself boiling water and grinding coffee. Desmond shouted something to her in a patois, and she stopped what she was doing and started to tear strips of material instead.

"My daughter," explained Desmond, proudly. "My wife," he added, pointing to the window, where they could see another lady pegging out washing. "Our son is out running errands. We're getting ready for Mardi Gras."

Picking up on the conversation, Desmond's wife came in from the back yard to help their daughter. "This is Odette," said Desmond. "My daughter is Esme. Our son is Gideon."

"It's nice to meet you all," said Toni. "You're being very kind."

"It's Mardi Gras," smiled Odette from the kitchen, as though that explained it and perhaps they wouldn't be so affable at any other time of the year. Her hair was braided and secured in a bun on the side of her head, probably ready for her own Mardi Gras headwear. As she moved around the kitchen she kept touching a feather boa with affection, which hung over a cupboard door handle.

Esme and Odette helped Desmond treat their wounds, bandaging what they thought needed bandaging and securing the bandages with some kind of tucked-in loop. Then Esme disappeared inside the house somewhere, and came back with shirts for both of them, trousers for Bart and a skirt for Toni.

"We'll wash your clothes for you," explained Odette, over coffee.

"You must let us pay–" started Bart, but Toni interrupted him, remembering Veronique the fruit lady's warning about them being offended.

"You're all very kind. We'd like to come back later and collect our things, if that's all right? You're all very busy and we need to... erm... find out a few things."

"What would you like to learn?" asked Odette.

"Well," said Toni, casting around for something that wouldn't freak them out.

"We need to get some provisions, and some souvenirs," said Bart, quickly. "It's not every day we turn up in New Orleans in Mardi Gras week. There must be lots for two strangers to town to see and do."

"Yes," agreed Toni. "And we need to get something for the Mardi Gras too. Would you recommend we start anywhere in particular?"

Odette and Desmond exchanged looks. "They've already decorated the streets. That's always nice to see," said Odette. "There are lots of food stalls, you can get something to drink too. And souvenirs are available in all the shops and on stalls."

"Please, go and have a look at our beautiful city," agreed Desmond. "Meet our beautiful people. Tell them Desmond sent you."

"And Odette," added Odette.

Toni and Bart washed themselves in a bowl of warm water. Odette took Toni's silky blue shirt and black waistcoat with care, and pushed everything over her arm with the taffeta skirt on top. Bart's outfit was so much more practical than hers – brown trousers, striped waistcoat, white shirt – it didn't need as much care. They changed into the clothes they'd been given, then they left the witch-doctor and his family to their preparations.

"What lovely people," said Toni, feeling much better just for being out of her bloodied clothes.

"I've always wanted to come to New Orleans," agreed Bart.

"I wonder what time we're in," mused Toni. "Everything looks very basic."

"But they have electricity, so it's not that long ago."

"There must be a newspaper we can check, or a sign advertising the Mardi Gras."

"I think that depends on when it is," said Bart.

They wandered the streets, necks stiff at all the leaning backwards to look at decorations hanging from upstairs windows, wrought-iron balconies, lamp posts and flag poles. Water hydrants, garbage bins, benches. Everything looked lovely and colourful. And everywhere they went, brown faces grinned at them, some shouted out greetings in one language or another.

"It's a good job I still have my schoolgirl French," mused Toni.

The money they had was US dollars, and it seemed good enough for what they wanted, the only attention being if they used a slightly higher denomination note.

They gazed up at the Spanish architecture and noted the Haitian and the Creole influences everywhere. The camellia was in bloom and even the streetcars were decorated for the upcoming festival. One stall had free gumbo on offer.

"We have to try this," said Toni, but Bart's hands already held a bowlful of the steaming hot seafood soup. And in the distance they heard the horn of a steamboat. "That must be on the Mississippi."

At one stall selling ribbons, Toni bought a couple – one for Odette and one for Esme. Simple but pretty. And she didn't know how else to thank them for their kindness without offending them. At another stall Bart bought them some more fruit. Desmond had seemed so happy with the mangoes, he assumed that was a good bet.

At the end of one street Toni caught sight of a fountain. She loved fountains. Everywhere they went, she always tossed a coin in the fountain and made a wish – more coins if the fountain claimed to raise funds for charity. She'd been doing that ever since the Trevi Fountain in Rome and it gave her a kind of link between each of the strange places.

"Come on, Bart," she called. "There's a fountain."

"We're not actually supposed to be enjoying ourselves, you know," he scolded. "We need to find out where in time we are, get the machine fixed, and get out of here."

"I know. But we also know that New Orleans was our destination. Perhaps the artefact has been here longer than we thought. And while we are here we may as well enjoy it. Soak up the atmosphere."

"Okay," he laughed, following her, but bumped into her when she stopped suddenly. "Whassup?"

She pointed towards the fountain. "Isn't that...?"

Chapter 4

CONRAD WAS SO BUSY negotiating with a chap with masses of beads around his neck he clearly didn't seen either Toni or Bart approaching him. He was dressed pretty much the same as Bart had been, but his waistcoat was leather, a red neckerchief hid the collar of his white shirt, and his trousers were black. Bart didn't wear a hat, but Conrad's was a black John Bull top hat with goggles strapped above the rim. Conrad also sported a pointy beard and a droopy moustache, but Bart was clean-shaven.

When they appeared at Conrad's side he almost jumped out of his leather waistcoat, dropping several strings of beads he was examining.

"Hey, Conrad," said Bart, pleased to see a familiar face.

"Oh. Bart, Toni," replied Conrad, nodding to them both in turn.

"What are you doing here?" asked Toni.

"I, er, came to find you two."

"Did we fall off the radar, then?" asked Bart.

"You've been gone for days."

"Days?" asked Toni. "We've only been here since this morning."

Conrad shook his head. "We lost contact with you about... four days ago. When you didn't report in the boss told me to come and find you. I didn't know where to start."

"You managed it, though," said Toni.

Ignoring her tone, Conrad looked them up and down, sending the bead-seller on his way and tucking his leather pouch into a pocket. "What happened to you two?" he asked. "Why the bandages? Is that a disguise?"

"No," said Bart. "We crash-landed." He explained how the machine had malfunctioned and how the fruit-seller and the witch-doctor had helped them so far.

"So you've already interacted with the locals?" asked Conrad.

"Well, yes," said Bart. "Why not?"

"You know we're not supposed to mingle, in case we change history."

"What were you doing with that bead-seller, then?" asked Toni.

"Er, buying beads?"

"Well, we were getting medical treatment."

"But your clothes?"

"They very kindly offered to clean them for us," she said. "We're to go back for them later."

"Anyway," asked Bart. "How did you know how to find us if you lost contact with us? We're not even where we're supposed to be."

"I was able to programme into your navigation system. We could see where we lost you and I took it from there. We knew where you weren't, at least."

"Lucky," said Toni.

"Where are you parked, anyway?" asked Conrad, glancing behind them as if expecting to see their machine there.

"It's out on the delta somewhere," said Bart. "We think it's where it was supposed to be, just a few years before where it was supposed to be was built."

Conrad made an attempt to follow that, but seemed to give up. "Can you take me there? More heads might help."

"Sure."

The three of them headed out of the town, towards where they thought the crash-landing site was. But they didn't have to look too hard. Toni had dripped blood on the dirt-packed track and the spots were easy to follow.

"Where's your machine?" Bart asked Conrad.

"I'm in a cemetery. I think it's the old cemetery. I was able to hide it quite well among the tombs."

The walk to the crash site only took them about twenty minutes. It took them a little longer to find the exact spot over the rougher ground. The poor thing looked very sad and dejected on its side.

Bart's time machine was a motorbike and side-car combination, usually garbed up to look like an old Triumph. They rarely went back before the old bike was originally built, so it suited their purposes quite well. Much of Bart and Toni's work was wartime work. This was actually the first time they'd ventured out of Europe, in fact, so the Triumph usually fit in quite well. As they were coming to America, they'd garbed it up as an old Harley.

While the boys took great pleasure umming and ahhing over the engine and other technological bits, Toni went into the side-car part of the machine to retrieve their stash of gold coins. They had a certain amount of currency with them that would have been in circulation in the 1940s, and so far they'd got away with using the coins. But the notes, with pictures of presidents on, might be more difficult. There would be a bank somewhere in the town where they could swap one of the gold coins for some local currency. Luckily, with the machine being in an unpopulated part of the country, no one had tried to mug it. And everything was still in its place, apart from the bits that had fallen off in the crash.

Conrad and Bart flicked some switches and checked the dials and Conrad asked Bart to repeat what had happened during the malfunction.

"I don't know what it can be," he said at last. "Perhaps the boss will know. We'll need to make contact with him, if we can find a communication portal. Or perhaps we can use my machine to contact him."

They agreed that might be the best bet, but with night falling they should find some accommodation first.

"Everywhere's probably fully booked, with it being festival week," said Toni.

"I bet Desmond would find us somewhere," said Bart. "He seemed like a nice bloke. Or your bead-seller?" he said to Conrad. But Conrad didn't reply.

"It looks like a mechanical failure," he said, instead. "We'll need to rebuild the steam pump first, I think. But we'll have to improvise. They won't have what we have in this era."

"Do you know what year it is?" asked Bart.

"It's 1926. You overshot by twenty-two years."

"Crikey," said Bart.

"Perhaps there's a library or a drugstore where we can get a newspaper," said Toni.

"And maybe a motel where we can stay," agreed Bart.

"You'd better get everything you need and then we'll head back," said Conrad.

Bart and Toni rummaged through the side-car and top box to get what they needed and Toni stuffed it all into a carpet bag. Bart threw a satchel over his shoulder and the three of them shifted the contraption to a more suitable place, covering it with scrub.

"It should be all right here," said Conrad. And the three of them headed back to town.

On their way past the end of the road, they made a quick detour to Desmond's brightly coloured door and knocked. Esme answered and, seeing who it was, called out to her father.

Desmond told her to invite them in, and Odette told them to sit down and have something to eat with them. It would have been rude to say no, so the three of them joined the family, now including Gideon. And they ate and drank and chatted about the upcoming fiesta.

"We could do with somewhere to stay," said Toni. "Can you recommend anywhere?"

"You will find plenty of hotels downtown," said Desmond. "They're likely to have room as there are so many of them there."

"But in case they're all full," said Odette, "Veronique, the lady who sent you to us, she has rooms. She doesn't usually let them out to strangers, but she's my sister and I'm sure she'll let you stay there for a day or so."

They thanked the family for their hospitality, took directions, and headed off downtown to find a hotel. Desmond had been right. There were quite a few and some still had vacancies.

"Will they accept our gold?" asked Toni.

"I have the right denomination notes," said Conrad. "But you might have to come in with me," he sneered, leering at her.

"Forget it," said Toni. "Either you two can bunk up or I'm in with my brother. There's no way I'm sharing a room with you."

"Suit yourself," said Conrad, resigned but accustomed to her rebuffs.

The hotel they chose had a lovely little courtyard behind it, but the fascia was on the street front. The French quarter was very pretty, clearly the oldest part of the town even if the town hadn't expanded across all of the Delta yet. The were able to get just the one room, but with two beds: a double and a queen. Conrad and Bart were to share the double. Toni bagsied the queen.

It was strange to be in a hotel with no television. There was an ancient contraption Bart assumed was a telephone, which was how they were to order room service. Conrad eyed the thing with interest anyway.

"We might be able to get hold of the boss with that," he mused.

Toni preferred to leave the technological side of things to the boys, and didn't care how unfeminist it was. Technology didn't interest her in the least, and quite often she thought she was actually better off not knowing how everything worked.

"We'll try your machine first, though," said Bart. "Wiring up that old phone might take up more time than we have. We usually only get 72 hours in any one place and we've already been here for a day. We don't know if we can complete our mission in this era, or if it will alter history. And we don't know yet how long it's going to take to get us away from here."

"I suggest we all get some sleep," said Toni, making herself comfortable in her borrowed clothes on the roomy bed. "We can have an early start in the morning while we try to figure everything out." And anyway, her head hurt and she needed to rest.

"I'm not turning in yet," complained Conrad. "I want to go and explore the bars. You coming with me, Bart?"

Bart shook his head. "Nah. I'm a bit shaken after the crash. I wish we had some paracetamol, but maybe we can send for some warm milk instead."

Conrad snorted. "Warm milk? You'd do better to sample the bourbon. That'd knock you out."

"Yeah, and give me a headache in the morning too. No, you go. I'm turning-in too."

As Conrad let himself out of the door, Bart called after him: "And don't wake me up when you come back."

Conrad closed the door softly behind himself, and headed on down the stairs.

Chapter 5

"I DON'T TRUST CONRAD," said Toni as soon as the door closed behind him.

"You just don't like him," replied Bart, eyeing the telephone on the bedside table.

"No, I don't. He's creepy and slimy and he gives me goose-pimples. But I don't trust him either."

"Why don't you trust him?"

"If he was truly looking for us, why wasn't he actually *looking* for us?"

"What do you mean?" Bart stopped staring at the phone and looked at her instead, puzzled.

"He was negotiating something with that bead-seller. He even had a handful of beads. And he looked as though he'd been here for at least a day, but he said he'd only just found us."

"He also said that we've been off the radar for several days, yet to us we've only been here one day. Time has already been warped a little. Perhaps it seems like just a day to him too."

"Why do you keep looking at that telephone?"

Bart picked the instrument up and examined all of its parts. "Conrad said we might be able to contact the boss. We'd need to adapt it a little, with whatever we can find. But he might have a point."

"I don't think there's anything you can do with it tonight," said Toni. "Get some rest and we'll see what we can do tomorrow.

DOWNSTAIRS IN THE BAR, Conrad was drinking bourbon and thinking. Something had gone wrong and he needed to fix it. He'd have to help Bart and Toni fix their time machine, but the artefact they had come for he needed to find first too. He'd figured he needed to get here before they did – about twenty-two years before, when the artefact was hidden in the first place. The wires must have got crossed somehow, and that's how they ended up here early too. Now it was a race to see who would find it first.

THE FOLLOWING MORNING Bart was woken by the sound of Conrad's snoring. He hadn't heard him come back, yet his snoring woke him up now. He looked across at his sister's bed and she was snoring softly too. An ornate clock on the fancy mantelpiece told him it was 8am. He was hungry and he needed breakfast. He tiptoed into the adjoining bathroom to get ready, and when he came out he softly shook Toni awake, a finger to his lips warning her not to wake Conrad.

Good as gold, Toni silently got herself ready and they crept out of the room and downstairs to where they found tables laden with fresh fruit for breakfast. They ate their fill, and took some for later too, then off they went on their quest.

"Where should we start?" asked Toni.

"How about we find the old cemetery where Conrad claims he left his machine?"

"What do you think he has it garbed as?"

"Probably a period motorcar if I know him," said Bart.

They purchased a primitive street map from one of the street vendors, got their bearings, and went in search of the old cemetery.

It was so easy to navigate the city as the roads were all in the classic American grid, meaning even if they did take a wrong turn, they could easily correct when they reached the other end as all streets linked to each other. With the mighty Mississippi behind them, they passed through two parks before reaching the walled cemetery. They shinned up the wall to get in as the wrought-iron gates were locked.

When they landed on the other side of the wall they stopped in awe of the maze of tombs, gravestones and mausoleums. It was like a little town in its own right, with paths criss-crossing all over the place, disappearing up dead-end alleys. Some of the tombs were new and well maintained, shining white marble in the February sunshine. Others had been allowed to fall into disrepair and the red bricks they were made from emerged from the stucco and paint.

The whole outside wall of the cemetery was lined with memorial stones and plaques. But the actual cemetery itself consisted of what looked like different-sized houses, some surrounded by polished and painted wrought-iron fences, others the fences had been allowed to rust and weather, but more were free-standing.

"Where on earth do we start?" said Bart, running a hand through his hair.

"We'll cover more space if we split up," suggested Toni.

"But it could be anywhere. The place is a rabbit warren."

"Start at the gate. You go left, I'll go right, and we'll just keep going until one of us finds something. How long can it take?"

Bart surveyed the cemetery before them. "It's huge."

"Then we'd best make a start," said Toni, logical and practical as ever.

So the two of them split up and went off in opposite directions, up and down the grid-work of paths, occasionally seeing each other at the other side as they turned and went down the next path.

Toni's side didn't reveal anything, but she did marvel at all the different architecture, the different standard of tomb or mausoleum or sarcophagus, depending on how wealthy or not the deceased or their family was. She was saddened by some of the dilapidated ruins, but any descendants had probably died out long before so there was no one to maintain them. Most, though, were in good order, painted in bright colours. Some had brickwork exposed behind plaques or stones that had come away – or been pulled away. But most were perfect examples.

Just as Toni was about to give up, she heard Bart shouting her name and she ran to the end of her path and waited for him to emerge.

"I found it," he panted, gesturing for her to follow him. He was about two-thirds of the way along his section, a well-kept well-maintained. She ran towards him and followed him back down his path.

There, in one of the older mausoleums, the double-width doorway stone was clearly already loose and pushed to one side. Inside the darkness there was no grave or sarcophagus, but there was a 1926 Model T Ford.

"See," said Toni after Bart told her what it was. "I told you he seemed to know exactly where he was, or he would have made it a later model."

"Hmm," agreed Bart. "I think you may be right."

"Sticks out like a sore thumb here, though," she mused.

"Perhaps he crash-landed too. But one thing's for certain, whatever he is here for, you can pretty much bank on it not being far from here."

The two of them examined Conrad's machine, but there was nothing left in it not secured down. The car radio was in place, which would be how he communicated with the boss. But there wasn't really anything they could nick or salvage to do something with the phone with.

"And we won't be able to contact the boss without Conrad's key," said Toni, gloomily.

"Oh, I don't know," mused Bart. "I might be able to hack into it. We have our own key..."

"Let's see what he comes up with by himself, give him the benefit of the doubt."

Bart was surprised. "That's very generous of you. More generous than usual."

"I'd rather give him a chance and be wrong than lay into him and be wrong."

They pushed the stone across the double-doorway again and made sure it didn't look disturbed, and then headed back to the main road.

They didn't get much chance to do anything else because there was a procession heading right towards them.

"It's not Mardi Gras already, is it?" asked Toni.

"No, we're definitely early for that."

"There's a brass band coming towards us."

"That'll be a funeral. We'd best move out of the way in case they're coming in here."

And, sure enough, the small band of about eight musicians danced their way slowly towards them, but they continued on past, followed by a huge procession, everyone also step-touching, step-touching in time to the bluesy mournful tune.

"Ah," said Toni, quietly, ensuring she still showed her respect. "The gate's locked on this one. There must be another one further up."

They fell in behind the crowd, step-touching in time with everyone else, and followed them a few blocks to another, larger, newer cemetery. This one had more space between the mausoleums and was better maintained too.

"See, now," said Bart. "Conrad knew exactly which cemetery to land in too. Yup, he's definitely up to something."

"We need to sort out a communication portal and get in touch with home," reminded Toni.

They started to head back towards their hotel, but noticed Conrad and the bead-seller coming towards them and, for some reason, Toni felt the need to hide.

"Come on, let's mingle with this funeral for a while," she said. "They might not see us."

"I wonder what they're plotting?" said Bart, shuffling along in time to the music, trying to get the step-touch at the right moment. Toni was much better than him.

"We'll find out soon enough."

Once they were sure Conrad and the bead-seller had rounded the corner, they set off again. This time, as they re-joined the main drag, they heard a telephone ringing in one of the buildings, but they ignored it. Until someone came running out and after them shouting.

"Hallooo! Hello! Antonia? Bar-tolamew?"

They turned to see a man running towards them waving his arms.

"How does he know our names?" whispered Bart.

"Telephone-ee!" the man cried "Telephone-ee."

"For us?" asked Toni.

"*Oui, oui.* Come now."

And so they went back with the stranger, who held out the old contraption for them, a candlestick-type version that you needed two hands to hold and use.

"Hello?" said Bart into the mouthpiece.

No answer.

"Hello!"

Static.

"HELLO!"

"Bart? Where the hell are you?"

"Is that you, boss?"

"Yes! Where are you?"

"We're in New Orleans."

The shop-owner watched on anxiously and Toni smiled at him, hoping to put him at his ease. He was trying to over-harken on the conversation, and they couldn't risk anyone knowing why or how they were there. She looked at the trinkets he had for sale, so that he was torn between selling her something and listening in on the phone call.

"Do you know the year?" asked the boss.

Bart waited until the shop-owner was engrossed with Toni before answering.

"Yes, it's 1926."

A pause. "Then you over-shot."

"How did you know how to find us?"

"I used your last-known co-ordinates and compared them to Conrad's. He's gone missing too–"

"He's here–"

"What?"

"He's here. With us."

"Now?"

"No, we left him in the hotel room but he's wandering around town now with one of the locals."

"Well, listen Bart, I won't have long,"

Already the static was kicking in.

Chapter 6

"I JUST TRIED TO GET you on Conrad's communication portal," the boss said. "I'd tried yours for days but was getting nothing, not even static. But I received information that you were close."

Bart said, "We'd just found where he'd hidden it but he has his keys and things with him, so we couldn't activate his radio."

More static.

"Sorry, boss? This is a terrible line!"

"Something's gone missing from (crackle, crackle) here. Something that could change the course of history if we don't get it back."

"What is it?" asked Bart.

"It's another amulet," said the boss.

"We haven't got it."

"I think whoever has it deliberately tampered (crackle, crackle) with your machine. The artefact you're looking for was placed in its hiding place at about the time that you're there now. If it isn't hidden, like it's supposed to be (crackle, crackle), if it's used, then... the course of history could change. That and the one that's (crackle, crackle) could prove fatal if they're ever reunited. If Conrad's there, he's the only (crackle, crackle) who could have taken it."

"Where was it hidden? The building we were supposed to land in hasn't even been built yet."

"It's (crackle, crackle...) shop (crackle, crackle...) crystal (crackle, crackle... crackle, crackle...)"

"Boss? Boss!"

Toni and the shop owner stopped looking at his wares to see what Bart was shouting at.

"BOSS?!"

"Has he gone?" asked Toni.

"I think so," said Bart, pushing up and down on the lever trying to get a response. But there was just static, and the person who owned the telephone thought he was going to break it.

He gave up and handed it back to the man, who looked expectantly at Toni, waiting for her to pay for the pendant she was holding.

She handed over some pennies, thanked him for the use of his phone, and they left the building. Bart filled Toni in.

"Looks like your suspicions were spot on," he said at last, when he'd finished.

"So someone, probably Conrad, stole this other artefact from our vaults?"

Bart nodded as they walked.

"Then he tampered with our machine to stop us landing in 1948, but the thing misfired and overshot us anyway by twenty-two years..."

"To when the artefacts were separated," continued Bart, "and one hidden now, here in New Orleans, and the other taken somewhere else."

"Then Conrad fixed his own machine to come back to now and reunite the two artefacts together?"

"He must have been furious when we showed up," said Bart.

"And perhaps that bead-seller knows where the other amulet is. The one Conrad's come for, the one we were supposed to rescue in 1948."

"He might have it already..."

"I don't think so. If he had both halves, then he'd either be doing what he wants to do with them or he'll be taking it back to the future–"

The two of them looked back towards where they saw Conrad and the bead-seller.

"That might be why he's making his way back to his machine," said Bart.

"Come on," said Toni, setting off at a trot.

Bart started to jog after her, but they pulled up again when they saw Conrad, alone, coming back towards them. And this time he saw them.

"Act as though we don't know," hissed Toni.

"Conrad!" said Bart, slowing right down to a standstill.

"What have you two been up to?" asked Conrad. There was no sign of the bead-seller.

"We've been looking for some kind of communication portal to get in touch with the boss."

"Any luck?"

"Nah. There's nothing here – just your machine. We could go there?"

Conrad shook his head. "I've just been trying to get in touch with him myself, but I can't get through."

"Really?" asked Bart, all innocence.

"Too much static. We can try again later if you like?"

"That'd be cool," said Bart. "Where are you off to now?"

"Just sightseeing. You?"

"Er, same."

"Enjoy," said Conrad, sauntering off.

And so they parted and went in different directions.

"He can't have found it yet," said Toni.

"Which means we still need to," said Bart.

"What did the boss say? Did he tell you where you might find it?"

"He said 'crackle, crackle, crackle' a lot."

"And?"

"That's it. Something about a shop. And a crystal."

"Our keys are crystals–"

"Maybe that's it," said Bart. "Maybe we can fashion a crystal to use Conrad's communication portal?"

"We could do with finding the one that Conrad brought with him, the one he stole," said Bart.

"Do you think he has it on him?"

"He might have given it to that bead-seller."

"Or it might be in the Model T."

Gosh, there were so many possibilities, and so little time in which to explore them all.

"And a shop that sells crystals," said Toni, aghast. "There are so many shops and stalls here that sell fancy goods like that."

"We need to sit down, take stock, explore all the avenues," said Bart, the analytical side of him taking over. "Otherwise we could be running around in circles getting nowhere."

"There's a café over there," said Toni. "Let's get some coffee, stop, pause, think."

TONI SAID, "LET'S PUT what we have in some sort of order."

Conrad had an amulet, Artefact A. It's the other half to the one they were looking for, Artefact B. If the two amulets were somehow put together, something terrible would happen that would change the course of history. In February 1926, the amulets were separated and at least one was left somewhere in New Orleans, but probably moved to a new location that hadn't been built yet but that would be there in 1948 – close to where they were supposed to land. There was a chance of the amulets coming together in or after 1948, which was why Bart and Toni had been sent to fetch Artefact B. They already had Artefact A in the vaults, unbeknown to Toni and Bart, but Conrad had stolen it and brought it back to 1926.

Conrad tampered with the controls on the Harley so that they didn't land in 1948, or even in New Orleans. But it had gone wrong. It still landed in New Orleans, but it overshot by twenty-two years. Meanwhile, Conrad had set his own Model T to go back to New Orleans in February 1926, and it had landed close to where Artefact B was in 1926.

That gave them both of the old cemeteries, the French quarter, and this part of the Mississippi...

"The Mississippi," said Bart, a light going on behind his eyes. "It's not in a building, it's on a boat. A steamboat."

"And the boat hasn't come in yet," said Toni.

"Or he'd already have it," said Bart.

"That's why he's hanging around."

"Perhaps it's late."

"I wish we had Google so we could look up the boats," said Toni. "Or at least a library."

"But there must be some sort of office where they keep information like that," said Bart. "The steamboats must run to a timetable."

"I bet they're all due in for Mardi Gras anyway," said Toni.

"Which we're only going to catch briefly before it's time for us to go," said Bart.

"The boats will all be here in time for the fiesta," said Toni. "There's no point them coming otherwise."

"There must be an administration office or something for the boats," said Bart.

"Let's go to the river, have a look there."

They finished their coffee, left some coins on the table, and headed off towards the mighty Mississippi.

As they reached the vast expanse of dirty, muddy, brown water, they breathed in the soily, earthy smell. It smelt like the first rain on parched earth, mixed in with brine. Toni took a deep breath and filled her lungs. It was almost like being at the seaside, yet this was a river. There were a few big boats moored up at various points, but there was still plenty of room for more.

Various wooden shacks lined the winding bank, general traders, coffee houses, already decorated for the approaching fiesta. The two of them wandered along, wondering which of the wooden shacks might house a harbour master. Instead, they found two old men playing jackstones in the dirt.

"Good morning," said Toni in French.

The men replied in Spanish. So Bart took over.

"Is there a boat late in?"

They exchanged some language that Toni didn't really understand until Bart thanked them and gave them each a coin for their help, a gesture that caused them both to grin, exposing cracked and missing teeth.

"What did they say?" asked Toni as they walked away.

"It's the showboat," said Bart. "She should have docked yesterday."

Chapter 7

THE SHOWBOAT WAS DUE in yesterday, but it had been delayed, that much they could pretty much glean from everyone. It had been upriver, performing at the various ports along the way. Whoever or whatever was on board could have joined the boat anywhere.

"What if it's someone fetching the amulet here?" said Toni to Bart.

"Yes, that could work," agreed her brother.

"We should concentrate on fixing the Harley," suggested Toni.

"The bike hadn't even been built yet," mused Bart. "It's a 1929 model. They might not have the part we need."

"Then, as usual, we'll have to improvise."

Bart thought deeply as they roamed the banks of the Mississippi. Toni chatted to the locals, asking each of them when they expected the showboat and who was on it. As it turned out, anyone could be on it, as anyone could hitch a ride back down the river if they wanted to, and if they paid for their ticket.

"I wish we had time to go up the river on a paddle steamer," said Toni, wistfully.

"If we find everything we need to and still have time, then we will," smiled her brother.

Some of the locals were French creole, some were Spanish, some were white, some were black. Most of them spoke English, and those who didn't, they could usually get by with Toni's schoolgirl French or Bart's university Spanish – he often said that Spanish was one of the easiest languages to learn.

Everyone was very friendly, very trusting, and very generous – with their time, their information, and anything they had that might be of use to someone.

A lot of the performers on the showboat would have family in New Orleans, and most would want to be back for Mardi Gras. Some would even be performing for the event or taking part in the procession. The riverside was going to be just as busy as anywhere else in the town.

Both cemeteries were fairly close to the river, so even if the amulet wasn't on board the boat, if it had something to do with someone on the boat, it could be hidden somewhere near to the river too.

But if there was a funeral, equally, the artefact could be hidden in one of the coffins. So another item on their list was to find out how many funerals had taken place recently and how many were due over the next few days. Probably none were booked in over the fiesta time.

As they made their way back up the bank towards the French quarter, they saw Conrad's bead-seller. He was selling beads but still moving at a pace.

"Shall we follow him?" dared Toni.

"You bet," said Bart.

They left the river behind them and followed at a good distance behind Conrad's friend.

He looked either mixed race or suntanned white, late twenties, with sore-looking eyes. A hint of a moustache touched his upper lip, but the rest of him was clean-shaven and short-haired. The beads he was selling were wrapped around his neck, hundreds of them in different shapes, sizes and colours, and different lengths too. Most were made of coral or pearl or other shiny stones. Some were all one colour, others had mixed beads on them.

The money he got for his wares he stashed in a leather money belt around his waist. He had a bit of a nervous tic that caused his head to flick back and his eyes to blink at intervals. But he was nifty on his feet.

He wore baggy blue trousers and a short-sleeved shirt, but more than that they couldn't really see.

When the crowds thinned out it became harder to follow him without being seen.

"Do you want to carry on without me?" asked Toni. "We might be less obvious that way."

"Sure, but what will you do?"

"I'll nip back to see Desmond and Odette, see if our clothes are ready. These are great, but it'd be nice to have a change, and I think my own outfit might be more suitable to a Mardi Gras anyway – it's a bit more... colourful."

"Okay. I'll see you back at the hotel at, say, three o'clock?"

They both checked their watches were reading the same time. Then Toni watched as Bart followed the bead-seller down another side street.

She navigated her way back to the witch-doctor's, and the family were very pleased to see her.

"Come in, come in," said Esme, taking her by the hand and leading her through into the magical grotto.

"I bought you this," said Toni, handing her the ribbons. And the child's little face lit up, the whites of her eyes and the white of her teeth almost luminous.

"It matches my dress," she said, scampering off to fetch her parents.

Desmond and Odette both came to see her, then Esme reappeared with a neatly folded pile of clothes.

"Thank you so much for doing this," said Toni.

"What have you been up to?" asked Desmond. And Toni filled them in on everything so far.

"Do you know when the showboat is due in?" she asked.

"It's late," said Desmond.

"It's usually here on a Tuesday," said Odette. That made today Wednesday.

"But it didn't turn up," continued her husband.

"There's a rumour someone was arrested in," said Odette.

"What for?" asked Toni, surprised.

"We won't know until it gets here," said Desmond. "But a lot of folk are annoyed."

"They're waiting for their relatives, or for things they've ordered from the other towns, or just to book a show," said Odette. "Are you wanting to see a show?"

"Er, yes. I think we do."

"Well, it might be here later today."

"What have you done with your brother?" asked Desmond.

"We bumped into some friends," said Toni. "He's off with one of them."

"That's nice," said Odette.

"Where are you staying?" asked Desmond. Toni told them.

"It's nice there, but expensive," said Odette. "You should think about speaking to my sister, Veronique."

"That's fine. We shouldn't be here that long. It's okay for a few days."

Esme came out of the kitchen carrying a tray with cups of coffee on and sweets on a plate. She'd already tied her new ribbon around one of her braids.

Toni stayed with them for an hour, chatting, learning about the showboat and the people who travelled on it. Then she had to be off to meet Bart and find out what he'd learnt, if anything.

Chapter 8

BART FOLLOWED THE BEAD-seller right out of the French quarter and into the larger city. He stopped to sell strings of beads to anyone who wanted them. Gradually, the stash of beads around his neck grew smaller and smaller and the leather pouch that dangled by his hip hung lower and lower with the weight of all the cash.

Bart kept at a decent distance, looking into the first shop or house window he passed if the bead-seller stopped and turned. He ended up buying bread and fruit from a couple of street-sellers and some feathers for Mardi Gras, and tucked them in the satchel he wore across his body. The food might come in useful, he thought. Toni might like the feathers to wear on Mardi Gras as they were royal blue, black and white and would look quite jaunty tucked into the rim of her top hat.

Gradually, the streets became less populated, the buildings less cramped together, until they opened up into a wider road with larger houses behind high walls on each side. Bart had to drop back further as his presence might be noticed.

The bead-seller continued on, but seemed to stop selling his wares the further he got from the tightly packed streets of the French quarter. Then, as he reached the gateway to a particularly grand-looking residence, he disappeared up an alleyway between this house and the terraced houses next door.

Bart lurked at the end for a short while, then he ducked down the alley in pursuit of the other man. It was much cooler down the alley and it smelled damp, a bit like how the river smelled but more subtle. Along the walls on either side at regular intervals was the occasional door or gate. Some were solid, substantial, sturdy. Others were just a bit of wood propped against the opening.

The bead-seller, about a a hundred yards ahead, stopped at one of the doorways, looked both ways quickly, then disappeared through the doorway. Bart slunk in one of the less-secure openings until he was sure the other mand was gone. Then he trotted after him, tried the big iron ring carefully, and swung the door inwards.

The door opened onto a lush, green courtyard that had potted plants around the outside and a giant pool in the middle. When the bead-seller emerged again from the building on the far side of the courtyard, Bart ducked behind a potted palm. The hawker had lost the strings of beads and instead was carrying a plate with what looked like meat on it. Then he took it to the edge of the pool and chucked it in in chunks.

For a moment, nothing happened. The bead-seller watched from a safe distance until the water started to bubble. Then three or four alligators suddenly appeared and started to thrash about amongst themselves, fighting over the meat. Satisfied, the bead-seller backed off a bit, then turned and went back inside the house, wiping his hands on his trousers and swinging the now-empty platter.

"Oh great," said Bart to himself. "Pet crocodiles. I don't think we need to upset him."

He waited for a while, not knowing whether to follow the man into the house. But as he hadn't really thought up any cover story, it was probably better for him to go away and come back again with Toni, if need be. She was so much better at coming up with viable cover stories on the spot.

But Bart couldn't just walk away without taking a closer look at the alligator pit. He'd never seen one before.

He kept one eye on the back of the house, that fortunately didn't have any windows in it other than the door, and one eye on the rippling water. He got as close to the edge as he dare.

The water was very clear and he could easily see that several tunnels led into the pool from elsewhere.

Bart looked up at the complex of housing that the tunnels went under. They could lead anywhere. The building was huge.

He heard shouting from within and made a quick getaway, but as he emerged into the alley behind the houses, he collided with another man who swore at him in Spanish.

"Sorry, sorry," Bart replied, also in Spanish. "Wrong address." He could feel the man's black eyes boring into his back before he turned at the end of the alley.

Chapter 9

TONI PACED UP AND DOWN outside the hotel waiting for Bart to show up. She was starting to worry.

On her way back to the hotel she'd popped into a few shops asking about a crystal amulet. She knew what it was supposed to look like as it was part of their brief – to make sure they didn't take the wrong thing and so possibly change the course of history. She assumed that its pair was a mirror image of it, so that the two would lock together.

Nobody could help her, although one person did say that someone else had also been looking for the same thing.

"Was it you?" she asked Bart, when they were finally reunited and they'd exchanged tales.

"There's only one person who could be asking the same questions as us," said Bart, shaking his head.

"Or two, actually, if you include his little bead-seller too," said Toni.

"Hmm, that's a point."

"We need to get to it before he does, and we need to get his away from him."

They went into their hotel so they could wash and change for dinner. Now they had their own clothes back they would feel so much more comfortable. But perhaps the borrowed clothes were better for exploring, and, of course, they'd stick out less obviously in the borrowed clothes. Bart might fit in quite naturally, but her frilly shirt and taffeta skirt were much more noticeable than the plain, non-descript, almost-rags-in-comparison clothes Odette had loaned to her.

Toni placed the pile of laundered clothes on one of the beds, her top hat pressed flat on the top.

"Is your torch working?" she asked. "So's mine," she added when he nodded his head. "We should get something to eat, then maybe we can go out exploring later?"

"Back to the bead-seller's place maybe?"

"Why not? That might be where the amulet is hidden."

"Or it might be where Conrad has stashed its counterpart," said Bart.

"I'm not sure I fancy those alligators, though," said Toni, wrinkling her nose.

"We won't be going diving," said Bart.

"Come on, then. Let's get ready and go and eat. I'm starving."

That reminded Bart about the bread and fruit he'd bought, but she wanted something a bit more substantial. So they got changed, went downstairs to eat, came back and got unchanged again, and then headed off to the bead-seller's pad.

IN THE DARK THE HOUSING complex didn't look quite so fresh and inviting. It wasn't very well lit, and now the sunshine had gone the greenery looked less green, more mud-coloured. The alley was more sinister. The doorway was harder to find.

But, they finally made their way there, tripping only a few times on the uneven ground. And they quietly let themselves into the courtyard behind the bead-seller's house.

"Is he in?" hissed Toni.

"I know as much as you do," whispered Bart.

"Does he live alone?" hissed Toni.

"I don't know."

"Has he gone out?" hissed Toni, but this time she was silenced by just a frosty look from her brother.

"Shall we go and have a closer look?" he suggested.

She nodded and then trotted behind him as he quietly negotiated the pool in the middle of the courtyard. She hoped the reptiles weren't hungry and was glad her wounds had stopped bleeding.

They reached the back door, but it didn't have a window in it after all. What used to be a window had been barred over and boarded up from the inside. And, as Bart had noticed earlier, there were no windows on this side of the house and there was no way around to the other side from here. The only way was to go through the house or walk all the way around. But they had no idea how far round they'd have to go and even if they'd know it from the other side.

"We'll just have to go through," said Bart.

"Is it open?" asked Toni.

He lifted the latch as quietly as he could. "Yup," he replied. He nudged the door inwards until he could see through the gap.

"It's a stairwell," he said.

They both pushed through to see several doorways leading off this inner courtyard and a stone staircase rising to more doorways off a landing.

"They look like flats," said Toni.

"Any one of them could be his," said Bart.

They had six to choose from – three on each floor.

As it happened, the downstairs rooms were actually storage facilities, one of which was very cold and had slabs of stone with various foodstuffs on them.

"This must be where he got the meat from," said Bart, nodding towards an empty bucket made of wood.

"This must be where they keep most of their food," agreed Toni, noticing the salt pigs and various other preservation methods and receptacles lying around.

They closed the door softly and tried the next one. This one contained beads, loose beads, strung beads, barrels and boxes of brightly coloured beads. The room was dominated by an over-sized table that probably served as his work area.

The third room contained sacking, barrels, pieces of wood, empty pots, and a few cast-iron implements that looked like weapons of torture.

"Perhaps this is what the usual everyday crocodile farmer uses to keep his pets trained," mused Bart.

"We must remember not to call them crocodiles," reminded Toni.

A door opened from above, and they heard the rattle of the door catch as it was pulled to behind whoever had come out.

Toni and Bart exchanged an alarmed look, then their eyes wildly scanned the tiny space for the best hiding place.

Bart nodded at some crates in a corner. They dived behind them as they heard the footfall on the tread of the stairs. There was no conversation, there were no cheery goodbyes. Whoever it was was on his own.

They'd forgotten to close the door properly behind them, so were able to spy on the stairwell and the doorway leading out to the courtyard. First they saw feet on the stairs, then the bead-seller emerged and noticed that the door was open. He stepped over, checked inside the room, and pulled the door to behind him.

Toni and Bart held their breath as they listened to him leave the lobby. When they thought he'd had time to cross the courtyard too, the crept out from their hiding places, Bart opened the door gently. No sign. He checked the other two doors. Still closed. He glanced up the stairwell. No sign of anyone. He beckoned to Toni that all was quiet and then loped across to the courtyard door, opening that a crack too to peer out into the night.

He just caught the outer door closing behind the bead-seller, and in the quiet of the night could distinguish footsteps going up the alley.

"He's gone," whispered Bart.

"What now?" she asked, creeping out of her hiding place.

Bart looked up the stairwell again. "He's gone out," he said.

"He may not live alone," she replied.

"He didn't shout goodbye to anyone."

"They might not do that here."

"We won't know unless we investigate."

Toni sighed. "Okay."

They tiptoed up the stairs, aware that there were three more doors off the landing that could lead anywhere or to anyone. The doors were numbered one to three, and each had a panel in the wall to the side with a doorbell and a name printed on a piece of card.

Mr and Mrs Franklin lived at number one. Hondo Pitts lived at number two. And Iniko and Jimiyu Lujan lived at number three.

"Crikey," said Bart.

"Did you think it would have his occupation printed on the card too?" asked Toni.

"No, but it would have been useful," he agreed.

"What do we do now?" asked Toni.

"Improvise," said Bart, knocking on the door of number one.

"You can't do that!" said Toni, as the door creaked open and a tiny, wizened face peered out.

"Hi there," said her brother, giving them the full benefit of his hundred-watt smile.

The face said nothing.

"We were told we could get some beads from here, for the fiesta?" he said, hopefully.

The face grew a bony, wrinkled hand and finger pointed at the door next door.

"Is that Hondo Pitts?" asked Bart.

The face nodded, the hand was withdrawn and the door was closed.

"Thank you!" shouted Bart at the closed door. Then he grinned at Toni.

"I thought you said you couldn't improvise," his sister grinned back.

"You're an inspiration to me," he replied.

They made their way to the scuffed red painted door that had a number two screwed onto it, and he knocked this one.

No answer.

He knocked again.

Still no answer.

"He went out," said a voice from behind them. It was the wizened face back at the open doorway. Then it closed again.

"Now what?" said Toni.

Bart tried the handle, and the door opened.

"You can't do that!"

"Why not?"

"Because that little old lady... man... has seen us. They might call the police."

"This is New Orleans," said Bart. "It's 1926. They probably didn't do that here then."

"But we can't just go in. What if he comes back?"

Bart thought for a moment. "That's a good point. Perhaps you could go and keep watch?"

"Downstairs?"

"In the alley. Soon as you think he's coming back, let me know and we'll hide again."

"Okay, but I don't like it," Toni sulked. But she made her way back down the stairs anyway.

Chapter 10

BART LET HIMSELF INTO the apartment, but there was no lighting. He could smell the remains of some incense that had been burning, or an aromatic oil. Or perhaps even a candle that had been extinguished. Whatever it was, it smelt like a Catholic church on benediction day, not at all offensive but disturbing all the same. He found a switch on the wall and flicked it on and off. Nothing. He had to rely on his torch to look around and it was already quite dark outside. It wasn't very clear, but he got the impression Hondo Pitts lived very sparsely. He didn't have much furniture, or not as much as the witch-doctor and his family.

Using his torch, Bart looked around the apartment as best as he could. There was some wooden furniture, a table, two chairs, a cupboard. Nowhere looked as though it would make a good hiding place, but all he needed was a box the size of a jewellery box.

A central ceiling light was covered with loose material that had a fringe on, but there was no lightbulb in the holder. Two windows looked out onto the front of the building. There were drapes up, pulled tight. A single door led to what was probably the bathroom, but otherwise the room was divided into sections with curtains and voile panels.

Bart pushed through some drapes that hung from the ceiling, separating the living area from the sleeping area. The bed was unmade but it looked comfortable enough. On a windowsill overlooking the front of the building was an ivory box. He opened it to find a few jewels in there – a bit of gold, some precious stones made into a necklace, and a cheap pendant on a leather thong.

He wondered if that was it. The pendant didn't look like anything special. It looked cheap but decorative. Bart grabbed it anyway and stowed it in a pocket for it was the only thing that even resembled an amulet in the box.

The window over the bed was a bit grubby and another drape hung there, but it wasn't drawn and he could see out into the street. There were a few people milling about, but one person coming towards the building looked familiar. In fact, Bart would recognise that John Bull top hat anywhere.

Conrad.

And he was heading his way. He might even be coming to see Mister Pitts.

Bart had to get out of there.

He ran to the door, careful to leave everything looking as he'd found it. He didn't think there was another entrance into the complex – or if there was it wasn't clear from the doors he'd seen so far. But if Conrad saw Toni lurking in the alley, he'd probably know why they were there.

In two strides he was out of the stairwell and into the courtyard. In the dusk light he found his way around the alligator pit and was at the outer doorway, making Toni jump.

"Conrad's coming," he hissed.

Toni looked up the alley towards where they'd come in, then she glanced in the other direction.

"I can't see him," she said.

"He was at the front of the building."

He guided her in the other direction along the alley, neither of them knowing where it went.

"What if he comes in this way?" asked Toni.

"There are plenty of doorways to duck into."

They hurried along the alley, but it didn't lead anywhere. There were plenty of doors and gates leading off, but the alley itself was a dead-end.

Turning around they went back the way they came, but as they reached the end of the alley, they could see Conrad and Hondo, and they were both coming towards them.

"Quick," hissed Bart, "in here."

He pulled her through one of doorways into another courtyard, this one less well-kept.

They closed the gate and leant their backs against it, panting for breath as quietly as they could. They could hear Conrad and Hondo talking as they passed outside, but then they heard another noise, a growl.

In the darkness, they heard a chain rattle and they saw a dog emerge from the shadows.

"Shit," said Bart. "I hate dogs."

"It's on a chain," Toni pointed out.

"It seems a very long chain," said Bart.

The Rottweiler barred its teeth.

As quick as they could they were out of that gate again and were relieved to see that there was no sign of Conrad and Hondo Pitts. They must have been safely back inside the bead-seller's house.

They ran to the end of the alley and continued running along the streets until they found themselves back on familiar territory. When they paused to catch their breaths, Bart told Toni what he'd found.

"I don't know if it's significant, but it might be what we're looking for."

"It might not even be anything," agreed Toni. But she also agreed that it was better for him to take it than to leave it. "So long as he doesn't notice."

Chapter 11

AS THEY ARRIVED BACK at their hotel, Toni and Bart were called to the reception desk.

"We have a telegram for you," said the concierge.

Toni and Bart looked at each other in surprise, and then at the concierge.

"For us?" said Toni.

The concierge handed them the yellow slip of paper.

TARGET NOT IN SHOP STOP NOT FOR SALE STOP
MIGHT BE IN BACK ROOM STOP

"What's he on about?" asked Toni.

"He could mean anything," said Bart. "Conrad's key. The artefact Conrad stole. The amulet we came for. The temporary key for our machine."

"But we already have at least one of those, probably," said Bart, holding out the amulet he'd found in the bead-seller's apartment.

"And that wasn't in a back room," said Toni, examining the trinket. She fingered the purple and white glass beads that had been set into the pendant and pulled a face. "No crystals here."

"But if we know what this is, it'll narrow down what the boss means."

"Okay," said Toni. "So we need to try out your amulet with the Harley first, then maybe with the Model T."

"Yes, come on then," said Bart, and they headed off out to the Delta first.

The weather was cool but dry and the walking kept them warm, and when they got to the crash site, Toni left Bart to fiddle with the mechanics of the time mechanism. That was his area of expertise. She just hung around, picking up debris, tidying up, looking out for passers-by.

Bart got the portable tool kit out of the locked top box and fiddled with the mechanics in the faring on the dashboard.

"This amulet doesn't fit anything here," he called to Toni over his shoulder. "But I think I've found where the lines were crossed or cut. I think I've fixed that now. Our own key might fit now."

"That's good," said Toni.

Bart fiddled some more, lifted the bike off its stand and rested it on the side-car wheels, and jumped on board. He jumped up and launched himself at the kick-start.

Nothing.

He tried again.

Still nothing.

He put the bike on its stand and had another fiddle, this time with the engine.

He kick-started it again, and this time it coughed a little.

"Might be a flat battery," he said. "If I can get it going it might be worth driving it round a little."

He tried again. This time it burst into life and he let it tick over as he revved with the throttle.

"Oh, well done," said Toni. "Do we go for a ride now?"

"We need to, but not too far as we need to conserve fuel until we can find where to get more from."

Toni climbed up behind Bart on the pillion. She didn't like riding in the side-car and only did that when they were travelling through time. She was much happier on pillion, and it was great to be able to ride without a helmet on. She loved to feel the wind in her hair. Their lids were in the side-car, and were more than just helmets. They had to wear those when they were travelling through time as well. They chose to wear their bike jackets, though. They were both starting to feel the cold a little. The leather flying jackets were comfortable.

"We can ride into town," suggested Bart.

"That'd be great," agreed Toni. "It'll certainly beat walking everywhere."

"Where should we park it?"

"The logical place would be one of the cemeteries, like Conrad has. We know he's already close to where we need to be."

"Okay." And within minutes they were back in town and driving around the city streets, drawing admiring and curious looks from the locals.

"Anyone'd think they'd not seen a motor vehicle before," shouted Toni.

"They have trucks," said Bart. "They must have motorbikes too."

"Yes, but this one hasn't even been built yet."

"They don't need to know that," said Bart.

When they stopped at a junction, some of the locals came for a closer look and smiled at Bart to show their approval.

"See," he said, as they pulled away again.

They paused outside the old cemetery. Bart left the engine running and went to inspect the lock on the gates.

"Conrad probably has a key for here," he said. "If he knew he was coming to this place, he'd already have everything he needed."

"Then the key to the gate will be on him."

"There definitely wasn't a key to fit this lock at Hondo's house."

"If Hondo has it, he might keep it on him too," said Toni.

"Perhaps they have a key each. Perhaps Hondo is also caretaker or something at the old graveyard."

Toni thought for a moment as Bart climbed back onto the motorbike. "Hmm, that would work," she said.

Bart opened the throttle and they drove around to the other cemetery. There were no funerals today.

"We need to find a suitable place to keep it," he said.

"I expect it would be fine at the hotel..." said Toni.

"They don't really have anywhere secure," said Bart. "I'd prefer to keep it hidden away, where prying eyes can't see it."

"There might be somewhere more suitable at the other one," said Toni. "But we need to go when the gate is open."

"Or get the key."

"Or get the key," she agreed.

"Let's check here first," said Bart. "They're still building these ones. There might be a mausoleum that's not properly sealed."

Once again they wandered up and down the new cemetery until they found one of the little buildings with the stone pushed to one side. There was no one inside, and it didn't look like they were expecting anyone any time soon. So that's where they hid the bike, pushing the stone across the opening and leaning it against the little building.

Back at the old cemetery they climbed the gates and headed towards where the Model T was hidden. Toni stood watch while Bart went in to investigate.

The Model T Ford had floorboards. One looked a bit uneven in this brighter light of day. Bart lifted it carefully and was delighted to have found Conrad's true stash – a medium-sized strongbox... that also needed a key to unlock it.

"Dammit," he said.

"What?" called Toni.

"Nothing is ever easy, is it?"

"What's happened?" she said, coming closer.

"I've found his safe," said Bart, holding the strongbox aloft.

"That's great," said Toni.

"It's locked."

"Oh, that's easy," she said. "If we take it with us I can pick that lock back at the hotel."

"But I need you to pick it here. We can't take it away. They'll know we've been snooping," said Bart.

"I don't really have any equipment here," she replied.

"Can't you improvise?"

"I'll try, but you'll need to keep watch."

"Let me try the pendant in his time travel mechanism first," said Bart. "Then we'll swap."

Bart had a bit more of a tinker with the mechanism in the dashboard, but shook his head.

"Nope."

"Then it must be one of the artefacts," said Toni.

"Either it needs taking back and putting somewhere safe," said Bart, "or it will be part of the repair for the Harley."

"At least we're narrowing it down," said Toni.

"Wouldn't it be nice, though, if everything slotted into place neatly," said Bart.

"Let me take over," said Toni. "I'll have a go at that box and you can keep watch."

They swapped places, but Bart soon got bored standing guard and instead went on another wander around the graveyard. Some of it was walled, some of the walls were incomplete. They were still building parts of the cemetery.

TONI TINKERED WITH the lock on the strongbox. She would have preferred to have her lock-picks with her, one of her favourite tools that was always handy. But that was back at the hotel, stashed away in the hotel room safe. All she had with her was a hat pin and a brooch pin. She'd just have to manipulate both of those.

After about ten minutes she heard the lock click.

"Yes!" she said with relief, and she punched the air in celebration. "God, I'm good," she said out loud for good measure.

The lid of the box sprung open and inside was Conrad's supply of gold coins, some paper money (very large denominations), some gemstones, and several cog wheels of different thicknesses and sizes.

"Curious," she breathed.

Hearing a footfall outside on the pathway, she backed out of the Model T Ford with the box in her hands and a smile on her face.

She scrambled to her feet and made her way to the door, saying, "You can thank me later but this looks very interesting," and she almost banged into a smiling Conrad, Hondo Pitts lurking behind him.

It took her a split second to glance behind them in search of Bart and then gather her faculties.

"I'll thank you now, if that's okay," said Conrad.

Chapter 12

BART SLOWLY MADE HIS way back to Toni and the Ford.

He started to whistle a tune, *When the Saints go Marching in*, but when he rounded the corner and saw Hondo Pitts standing outside the Model T Ford's mausoleum, his feet crunched to a standstill on the path and he ducked behind the nearest gravestone. He needed to think quickly.

"Hey!" he called out to Hondo Pitts.

The bead-seller looked up to see Bart coming towards him, and frowned.

"Is that Bart?" he heard Toni say from inside the tomb. And she emerged with Conrad in tow, but she was still holding the box.

"I told Conrad you'd gone looking for him," she said quickly. "But I managed to open it anyway." She turned to Conrad who was looking very puzzled. "I didn't think he'd find you in time and I wanted to get the key back to our machine before dark."

Picking up on her thread, Bart improvised too. "So you just broke into his box?" he said, shocked. To Conrad, "Sorry mate. I told her to wait, but you know what she's like."

Conrad looked from Bart to Toni to Hondo to Bart again and his frown matched the bead-seller's.

Toni flashed him one of her best hundred-kilowatt smiles, and presented him with his box, which he snatched from her hands, quickly checked the contents, and slammed the lid back down.

He stayed silent as he placed the box back in its hiding place, ignoring Bart's questions.

"Did you get in touch with the boss? Any idea on how we can get our machine going again? Do you know how close we are to finding our amulet we were supposed to get?" And so on and so on, but Conrad didn't answer.

He was clearly cross with them, but if he was allegedly on their side, he couldn't admit that they'd annoyed him or were doing something wrong. Not until he'd found what he'd come for himself first.

Bart grabbed Toni's hand and pulled her away.

"Did you get it?" he asked hopefully as they backed away. Toni nodded.

"WHAT DO YOU WANT TO do about them, boss?" asked Hondo Pitts, looking after them and lighting a cigarette.

"I don't know yet," replied Conrad.

He wondered why they were mooching around, what Toni was doing breaking into first his car and then his strongbox.

Of course, it was quite natural for them, he supposed, to think he wouldn't mind them mooching through his stuff to see if he had anything they could use to fix their own machine.

"They could have asked," he muttered.

"She did say he'd gone to find you," replied Hondo.

Conrad grunted.

"And they don't know yet of your plan to leave them here—"

"Don't even say that out loud," he growled. "Knowing that pair they might be lurking around the next tomb, listening in."

"Sorry, boss," said Hondo.

"And don't call me boss," said Conrad. "Not while they might hear you."

"Sorry boss."

"So long as you still have my amulet safe," said Conrad. "We just need to wait for the match to come in with the boat – or the person on the boat – and then we can dispose of those two. We still need them for now, though."

He turned back to his Model T Ford and checked it was secure. He pushed the floorboards back over the strongbox, now locked, pulled the stone back over the opening, and turned in the direction Toni and Bart had headed in.

"If we fall out with them over this they'll get suspicious. Just carry on as if nothing has happened. We need to see if that damn boat has come in yet."

And off they went towards the port.

"THAT WAS CLOSE," SAID Bart, rushing towards the main town centre again.

"Where were you?" Toni demanded.

"I got bored. There was no one coming and nothing going on in that graveyard. It was only a little wander. They must have literally followed me around the corner."

"It could have got messy, Bart," said Toni.

"I know and I'm sorry but there's no need to go on about it. You talked your way out of it easily enough." Toni nodded her head. "What did you say to him?"

"Just that we were waiting for him but didn't want to lose the light so you went looking for him, but in the meantime I thought I'd have a fiddle and it popped open, just like that."

"And he believed you?"

"I don't know. I don't think so. But he could hardly show his hand, could he?"

"That must have killed him, keeping his mouth shut."

"He went red, though. I thought he might pop," laughed Toni, her bad mood forgotten.

"Still," she said, "I could have been in trouble."

Bart was about to tell her to give it a rest when a deep-throated steam whistle sounded behind them. They turned towards the river.

The whistle sounded again.

"The showboat!" they both said at the same time. They turned on their heels and dashed towards the Mississippi, as excited as two small kids seeing their first paddle steamer.

"Well, it is our first paddle steamer," said Toni, reading her brother's thoughts.

They couldn't get there quick enough.

When they arrived at the river front there was a lot of activity as one of the biggest boats they'd ever seen on an inland waterway nudged towards its dock.

"Wow," said Bart.

"It's beautiful," said Toni.

And they both joined the melee at the dockside. It was like a mini Mardi Gras just welcoming the boat back to port, with flags and whistles and cheers and music.

"They do love their music," said Toni, delighted.

A crowd of children dashed to the gangplank, hoping to see or touch one of their idols. The smart ladies and gentlemen of the company gathered on deck until they were ready to disembark, waving at the people who had come to see them. But they weren't on a usual tour. They weren't performing to a bunch of strangers. These passengers were coming home. They were coming to help their friends and family celebrate the most important day of the year for the community.

"I see Conrad and is oppo are already here," said Bart, almost as an aside.

The pair were lingering by some crates and barrels, smoking woodbines.

"I wonder if Hondo knows he's from the future," mused Toni. "I wonder if Conrad brings him Benson & Hedges."

"I think that would comprise 'altering history'," said Bart, "And anyway, you're assuming they already know each other. They might have only just met on this particular trip."

"True," agreed Toni. "Worth a thought, though."

"He could fetch modern cigarettes as a bribe, though," said Bart. And he turned his attention back to the boat's arrival.

The paddle steamer had docked now and the passengers were getting off at one end while porters removed luggage at the other and friendships were rekindled while others greeted family members.

"It must have been a very grand life," said Toni.

"It still is, for these. This is now, remember. We're not in the future anymore. This is the past."

They watched the arrivals for a little while longer, watched the business of bringing a boat home to dock.

"Did you get anything out of Conrad's strongbox?" asked Bart.

"A couple of cogs, funnily enough."

"Cogs?"

"Yes. I'd just spotted them when Conrad walked in on me. I turned around to show you, but it was him. I didn't realise."

"They sound perfect," said Bart.

"That's what I hoped," said Toni.

"Should we take them back to the hotel or back to the hotel, do you think?"

"I don't think we should leave anything at the hotel, and I don't think Conrad realises yet that we've brought the Harley back. It might be best if we stash them in our own security chamber. He doesn't know the bike is here yet, so unless he goes out into the delta looking for it, everything might be safer with that."

"We just need to make sure he doesn't follow us to our own hiding place," agreed Bart.

"It probably wouldn't take him long to work it out."

"Hopefully we'll be gone by then."

"Let's go back to the Harley then, and make sure he's not following us," said Toni.

"Or Hondo," said Bart.

"Or Hondo," agreed Toni.

Chapter 13

CONRAD WAS LOOKING for someone in particular and he kept his eyes peeled on the boat. He scanned all of the faces, but didn't see the one he needed. So he asked one of the porters.

"Boy!" he called out. The baggage handler stopped in his tracks and turned to see Conrad.

"Yes, boss?"

"Halima Dominique? Is she on board?"

"Yes, boss. Miss Halima, she on the boat."

"Thank you," he said, pressing a coin into the boy's hand.

He turned to Hondo Pitts. "You follow those two," he said, nodding towards Toni and Bart's retreating backs. He'd spotted them almost instantly, but pretended not to. "I'll wait for Miss Dominique."

"Okay boss," said the bead-seller. Fortunately, he'd discarded his mound of beads for now so wasn't as noticeable, and probably more nimble on his feet. Conrad watched him go after the other two. Then he leaned against a bale of something or other and lit another Woodbine. The things got on his wick. They were bitter all right, but apart from that, the filter-less tips meant he kept getting tobacco on his tongue. He missed his Marlborough Lights, but he'd never get away with smoking those in public.

Above, there was a crack of thunder and a flash of light and the river started to whip up a bit. There was a storm coming. Conrad pulled up his collar, pushed down his sleeves, and thrust his hands into his pockets, the Woodbine stuck to his bottom lip. His hat would give him some protection from the rain and hopefully he'd finish the cigarette before it got too soggy. He pressed himself against the bale and waited.

Halima Dominique was the original owner of the two matching amulets. But they'd retrieved one of them – his one – many years after from a museum before the museum got pulled down. The other one, the one the terrible twosome were after was still part of her personal collection at this point. But it was at the 1926 Mardi Gras that she was to be robbed and the other amulet taken from her and eventually placed where Toni and Bart were supposed to find it twenty-odd years later. In 1926, though, the amulet was apparently buried with the rest of the stash somewhere in town before being moved out to the cellar of a house that hadn't even been built yet, which would be roughly where the Harley Davidson had come in to land. At the moment, it was still the Mississippi Delta. But New Orleans was a town that was to spread out further leaving, eventually, just a pocket of the original landscape in what would be a nature reserve by the twenty-first century.

Conrad had done all of this research back home. So he knew he could intercept the amulet now, before it was buried. Or even after it was buried but before it was moved out to the new town.

The Woodbine he was smoking was almost finished, so he lit another with the dying ember of the first and waited some more. Fat spots of rain started to fall onto the dry earth and another crack of thunder ripped the sky apart with a flash of lightning. The mixed smells of wet rain on dry grass and packed dirt drifted up and he breathed it in with the Woodbine smoke, just as he was racked with a fit of coughing that made his eyes water and he had to spit out the cigarette.

Then, after all the fuss had died down, she was there, slowly emerging from her cabin. Such a shy little thing for such a famous personality. Or maybe she wasn't so famous in those days... these days, as she would become in the future.

He finished his fag and stubbed it out with his boot, pulled his John Bull down over his eyes and put his hands back into his pockets.

Miss Dominique looked up at the sky and went back into her cabin, returning with a big black umbrella. It was old and worn with one of the arms broken and it probably doubled as a walking stick, but it did the job and covered her head enough for Conrad to follow her at a safe distance and not be seen. Unfortunately, that was also how she would be robbed – because she couldn't see her assailant coming.

For a moment Conrad wondered about doing the assailant's job for him. It would be so easy for him to simply relieve her of the trinket and she'd never be able to identify him. But that would probably change the course of history and despite everything, Conrad never, ever did that. As a rule.

And so he waited. And watched.

Halima Dominique wore a coat over her dress, but it gaped to reveal the black satin flapper drop-waisted dress she wore. She was fair for a creole, which had probably helped her become a showgirl, and she was pretty too. Her hair had been permed straight and she wore it curled and to the side of her face, with a flower tucked in at the top. She was wearing stockings that were getting splashed by the rain bouncing off the dirt, and the high-heeled shoes weren't really very practical for this kind of terrain. But he supposed she had an image to maintain.

He followed her at a very safe distance into a less savoury part of town and it was while she passed a saloon bar that he noticed who he thought might be her attacker. And he reminded himself again that he wasn't allowed to interfere. She had to have this mugging, she had to be robbed, and she had to end up in a hospital. But she recovered, and that was the main thing.

What he wasn't expecting, however, was the blow to the back of his own head. And he landed with a thud on the wet ground.

Chapter 14

BACK IN THE FRENCH quarter, Toni and Bart were semi-aware of Hondo following them.

"I bet they did see us," said Toni, looking behind them.

"We don't have much time," said Bart, looking up at the darkening sky. "We're about to have a cracker of a thunderstorm too."

"We'd probably do better if we split up again," said Toni. "And then if Conrad and Hondo are following us, they'll have to split up."

Lightning cut across the sky and was accompanied almost immediately by an almighty clap of thunder. Toni scurried into a doorway and Bart followed her.

"We don't even know where to start," he complained.

"The boss said a back room, so we need a building. A house or a shop."

"But where do we start?" asked Bart, throwing his hands in the air and ruffling his own hair again.

"We'll just have to watch and wait and see," said Toni. "But we can't go back to the Harley yet. Not if someone's following us. We don't want them to know we've already retrieved the bike."

"Give me the cogs, then," he said. "I can carry them in my satchel, and they're less likely to think I have them if they caught you red-handed."

The rain started to fall and a chill fell on them too as they both wrapped their flying jackets closer to them, grateful that they had them now at least.

"We'll just have to wander around, look at things, see what looks likely," said Toni.

"But it might not even be this part of town."

"Then one of us will have to go back to the boat and see if anyone suspicious seems to be getting off."

"They'll all be off already by now, I imagine, Tone."

"We have to start somewhere."

"Okay, you go back to the boat and I'll make my way back to the hotel. There might be another telegram waiting for us–"

"I doubt it, Bart. He's not used the same method of contacting us twice yet. I think his next message might be in a different form."

"But what?"

They both thought for a moment. He'd used the telephone. He'd sent a telegram. There was only one thing left that had been invented by 1926. Well, two things, actually.

"A newspaper," said Toni.

"A radio," said Bart, at the exact same time.

"A radio!" agreed Toni. "And the parts might also come in handy."

"The parts might be exactly what we need," agreed Bart.

"Okay," said Toni, "I'll go back to the boat and see if I can find a newspaper on the way. You work your way back to the hotel, in case he does send a telegram, but see if you can find a radio. Even if you need to nick it."

"They might notice, Tone," said Bart.

"Not if they're already busy with Mardi Gras preparations," said Toni, "Or the boat coming in."

Toni headed back the way she came – and almost collided with Hondo Pitts.

"Well, hello," said Toni to the bead-seller. "I almost didn't see you there without your beads."

Hondo grunted something back and pretended to be going somewhere else.

Toni backed away and waved cheerily at him. "See you later," she said.

Hondo grunted.

DAMN! SHE'D SEEN HIM. AND they'd split up. How was he going to follow them now?

He called a young black boy over and gave him a dime. "Follow that lady, will you?" The boy nodded. "Come back and tell me where she goes, and there's another dime for you."

"Yes 'm," said the boy, running off at a trot after Toni.

"Don't let her see you!" Hondo shouted after him, and the boy waved over his head and slowed down. Then he set off after Bart.

Hondo Pitts was annoyed. It was raining and all he was wearing was a short-sleeved shirt and a thin pair of trousers. There was no wide-rimmed hat for him to keep off the rain. No collar to pull up around his ears. No warm coat to huddle inside. He glanced up at the sky and cursed silently. But he kept at a safe distance behind Bart.

He turned to check on the boy and saw him disappearing around a corner after Toni. Then as he turned into the street Bart had just gone into, he saw the back-end of him disappearing into a store.

TONI WAS SURE THAT she'd lost the bead-seller but, even so, she took a very roundabout way of getting back to the port, keeping an eye out to see if anyone was following her. She was certain that they weren't, so off she headed.

When she got to the boat it was completely dead. Everyone who was getting off had got off and even the crew were taking a rest before getting the vessel water-worthy again. There was not a soul.

She was able to creep up the gangplank without anyone stopping her, and she felt the ground become unsteady beneath her as she did so. The rain wasn't helping. The water was getting quite choppy. And the boat was starting to dip slightly from side to side. She worked her way around the deck, trying doors that were locked, peering through windows that had blinds up at them or it was too dark inside to see anything. She identified an engine room, a laundry room, the captain's quarters, a bar with a stage at one end, a restaurant, and various other closets, broom cupboards and washrooms.

On the next deck down were the more residential cabins and lounges. The lounge doors were open, but all the others were locked. Not like the rest of New Orleans in this era, it seemed. But perhaps they had more experience of crime when they travelled so far though the whole country. It didn't do anything to help Toni, though.

She wondered about visiting the rest of the boat but decided it was a waste of time. So she made her way back to the riverside again, where it was raining heavier than ever and the only person she could see was a small boy sheltering under a shelter thing...

She smiled at him but he looked the other way, at what she had no idea. She started to approach him, but he took fright and scarpered into the advancing night. Then it occurred to her that the bead-seller might have set him on to following her.

"Interesting," she muttered out loud.

At a loss for what to do next, she went back to the hotel. Bart would be there presently. She may as well already be ready.

But when she got back to their room, someone had already been there.

Chapter 15

TONI LOOKED AROUND the room, cautious that someone might still be there. The beds had both been overturned, the mattresses pulled to the floor, slashes everywhere pouring out stuffing. The drawers had been upended and strewn across the room, the contents spilled on the floor. A mirror had been broken. She crept to the en-suite bathroom where the sight was much the same, but with toiletries squeezed out of tubes and soap trampled into the floor.

They'd been right not to leave anything of value here, even the gold coins they'd kept on their persons.

As Toni walked around the room her feet crunched on broken glass and she was grateful for her boots.

She checked that nothing of even any low value had been taken, then she lifted the telephone.

"(CRACKLE, crackle, crackle...) hello?" shouted a voice from the other end. It sounded as though he was calling from a long, long way away.

"Boss? Is that you?"

"(Crackle, crackle...) Toni...?"

"Yes, it's me!"

"Are you all right... (crackle, crackle, crackle)?"

"Yes! But how did you know?"

"I called and someone answered, then (crackle, crackle) heard a kerfuffle... (crackle, crackle, crackle...) slammed the phone down."

"We weren't here."

"Someone was... (crackle...) a scream... (crackle)."

He started to fade.

"Boss? BOSS!" But she lost him.

She pressed the receiver in a few times until someone answered again.

"Boss?"

"Switchboard, can I help you?" said the accented voice.

"Oh, er, someone's been in our room. I need to report it."

"I'll send someone up," said the voice.

"Thank you–" said Toni, but there was just a click and a dead tone again from the other end.

She looked around at the carnage, hoping they didn't think that she'd done it. She started to tidy up, automatically. But then she realised they needed to see this. So instead she perched on the edge of one of the beds and waited.

BART WAS LOOKING FOR a radio. He knew they'd have them, the museums were full of 1920s radios. But would they have them in 1920s New Orleans? And where did he go if he wanted to buy one? There must be shops and stores here that sold those kinds of things. He found plenty of food shops and lots selling crystals and amulets and voodoo dolls and all sorts of mumbo jumbo like that. But he couldn't find a Currys or a PC World or anything close.

"Guess I'll just have to pinch one," he murmured to no one in particular.

He'd seen Hondo Pitts ages ago. Blinking idiot should stick to selling beads. He was a rubbish tracker. Bart did wonder where Conrad had gone, though, and hoped he wasn't after Toni. She was cute, though. She'd notice if she was being followed, especially if it was by someone she knew.

Bart carried on going from store to store, and every store he went into, he also checked for a back room. Most were just single room properties, though – or only the one room was visible. But as the shopping area made way to residential, he did find himself sneaking a look into front windows too.

Nothing. He couldn't see a single radio. Plenty of the houses had back rooms... Hmm, now there was a thought. What if whatever the boss wanted them to find wasn't in a shop or store at all? What if it was in someone's home? Or even a run-down empty property? God, that opened up almost the whole of the city! They needed more information. They couldn't keep going on supposition and second-guessing.

They needed a proper strategy:

1. Find the crystal or the amulet or the whatever to fix the time machine on the bike.

2. Get the bike fixed and ready to go.

3. Find the amulet they'd been sent for? If it was already here.

4. Confirm the one they had was Conrad's.

Hmm, perhaps the one they had was the one they were supposed to find? Perhaps Conrad's was the one that they needed to find?

No, that didn't work. The boss definitely said that Conrad had already taken the one from the archives to match up with the one they were supposed to find. That meant he already had it with him when he came to New Orleans. But he might have given it to the bead-seller for safekeeping.

He went back in his mind and scrubbed out no 4:

4. Confirm the one they had was Conrad's.

He needed a proper piece of paper for this...

Huh, then he realised that maybe the amulet he'd stolen from Hondo's apartment wasn't the one Conrad had at all, but maybe another one?

4. Find out which amulet the one they already had was.
There, that was better.
5. If they find two amulets, see if they match together.
6. Take the booty, grab the bike, and get the hell out of New Orleans.

Oh, he wished he had a piece of paper.

As he looked around he realised he didn't recognise where he was at all. The whole area looked unfamiliar. That's what daydreaming and not paying proper attention did.

He stopped and turned a full circle and scratched his head. His thick brown hair was damp and itchy. He started to retrace his steps, sniggering as he passed Hondo lurking under a nearby tree.

Bart was lost. He needed to get back to the hotel. His stride got longer but he was aware of the bead-seller almost running to keep up.

WHAT JUST HAPPENED? wondered Hondo Pitts. He'd watched... Bart, was his name? He'd watched Bart have a whole internal argument all by himself, and then he'd spun on the spot and headed back in the direction they'd just came. He seemed to have some wind beneath him too as Hondo had to hop a bit to keep up. And still manage not to be seen.

He'd followed him in and out of shops. He'd watched him looking in folks' windows. What was he looking for?

The rain got heavier, and Hondo Pitts never liked to be out in the rain for very long. It made him shrink. He wasn't a fan of thunder and lightning either and here he had it all. Not a great day for the great Hondo Pitts.

He loped after Bart, trying to dodge raindrops and being seen. Mister Conrad would owe him for this, but it beat selling beads to people who didn't want them.

Chapter 16

CONRAD LAY FACE DOWN in the rain, mud seeping into his clothes and a lump growing on the back of his head. As he came to, he wondered briefly what had happened, but then he remembered as he pulled himself up.

He was following Miss Dominique – in the rain, clearly – and then the lights had gone out.

As he climbed to his feet, one hand instinctively went up to the back of his head, and he looked around in alarm.

But there was no one there, and even Miss Dominique had disappeared.

Well, that was shit, wasn't it?

And he too was lost somewhere in New Orleans.

And he was cold.

He made some attempt at brushing himself down, took one more look around him at the run-down area, then turned to head back to the hotel. All he could do was retrace his steps and hope he'd get there in the end.

At least the rain was starting to stop now, although he was soaked through to the skin and very cold. And stiff. This wasn't good. This wasn't very good at all. Everything was going wrong.

THE HOTEL MANAGER CAME to see Toni, along with a couple of heavies she didn't know. They had a look around, but didn't ask her any questions. Instead, the manager picked up the phone and spoke in French to whoever answered.

He's told them to fetch the police, thought Toni. Perhaps waiting like a good little girl wasn't the best idea she'd had. She should have cleared out while she had the chance.

What worried her more, though, was the two heavies. Especially when they stood in front of where she sat, took on an intimidating stance, and effectively blocked any hope of escape she might have.

She was here for the duration.

At least for now.

AS BART WALKED ALONG the corridor to their room he became aware of a bit of kerfuffle.

"What's happening?" he asked a maid who was making up the beds in a different room.

"The young miss n mister had their room burgled," she replied, not pausing in her task.

He thanked her and continued along quietly, creeping to the open doorway and peering in. Through the open door he could see Toni sitting on the edge of one of the beds. She was watching two big burly guard-types when she caught his eye.

Bart pressed a finger to his lips, "Shush."

Toni nodded almost imperceptibly, and her eyes slid back to the guard directly in front of her.

Bart kept as close to the door frame as he could without revealing his presence, wondering what had happened and how he could get Toni out of there.

On the wall behind him was an old-fashioned fire alarm... well, it may have been state of the art in present day New Orleans. But it was one of those round red things with a handle that turned around the outside.

He turned back to the open doorway and waited to catch his sister's eye again. When she did glance at him, he wiggled his eyebrows in an attempt to convey to her that he had a plan and she was to get ready to move.

To give Toni her due, although she clearly didn't know what he was doing, she managed to keep her face and her expression completely blank. Her eyes slid back to her captor. She didn't blink an eyelid.

Bart had to trust that she'd understand what was happening. In two strides he was at the fire alarm. He cranked it twice so that the bell sounded, then he ducked into the other open room where the maid was still cleaning and tidying.

Her face looked startled and she paused mid-pillowcase, giving him a quizzical stare.

"Fire?" said Bart, and comically shrugged his shoulders. He took the pillowcase from her and guided her out, and once she started to drift along the corridor with other confused-looking residents and staff, he ducked back into the room and hid behind the door jamb.

From here, if he peeped around the doorway, he could see the activity in his own hotel room.

First to emerge was one of the guards he'd seen watching Toni. He was followed by a management-looking chap – well, he was wearing a suit, so Bart made the assumption – and a hesitant Toni. The other guard-type person followed in the rear.

The four of them started to head towards the main entrance when Toni said: "Oh, I just need to get my handbag..." and she slipped past the second guard and back into the room.

The guard didn't know what to do, so Bart showed himself and engaged him in conversation, leading him along the corridor with the others. As they reached the stairwell, he said: "I'd best go back, make sure she gets out safely. You go on with the others."

The guard paused, looked puzzled, and looked back up the corridor before looking back at Bart, who nodded and winked. Then he followed his colleagues back down the stairs.

Bart made sure they'd all gone before dashing back to their room, almost bumping into his sister who was already on her way down.

He stopped her in her tracks, spun her round on the spot, and walked her back the way she'd come.

"Ah, so the fire alarm was you?" she said.

"Of course," he shrugged.

"We've been mugged," she said.

"So I gather," he replied.

Chapter 17

HONDO PITTS ARRIVED at the hotel just as everyone else was leaving and didn't understand what had happened or why everyone was hanging around outside in the pouring rain. He lurked for a bit. But there was no sign of Bart. Or his sister.

He looked around for the boy he'd set on after Toni and saw him sheltering beneath a nearby tree. Hondo went over to him and the boy told him what he'd seen the woman do but that she'd seen him so he ran off. He'd stayed close, though, and she'd come into the hotel ages ago. The fire alarm had gone off not five minutes ago. No, he didn't know the man Hondo asked about.

Hondo gave the boy another dime and off the lad tripped.

He waited around for as long as he decently could, but when the residents were advised that they could go back in, he realised that staying here was futile. The fire alarm had quite clearly been a false-alarm and he didn't need any prizes for guessing who might have set that off. They'd be miles away by now if they'd left from a different exit.

He watched as the residents all piled back into the hotel, then he circled the block to see if there were any rear entrances or windows they could have sneaked out of. There was a trade entrance that probably led to the kitchens, and a whole bank of windows, most of which were closed. And those that were open weren't really big enough for anyone to squeeze out of, other than perhaps a child.

If they came out this way, it would be the trade entrance.

He started to make his way inside, but was shooed away by a member of staff. If he wanted to search the hotel, he had to go in through the front entrance.

He completed his circuit of the block and followed the other residents into the hotel. Then he realised he neither knew which room they'd be in nor what name they were booked in under. He knew that Mister Conrad had booked the room too, but he didn't know his surname either.

Pitts took one last look at the reception area, then left the building. He'd have to go in search of Mister Conrad and tell him what had happened. He wasn't happy at having to go back out in the rain again.

CONRAD KEPT ON LOSING his bearings and was having dizzy spells and blurred vision. He concentrated on putting one foot in front of the other and hoped he was going in the right direction.

The rain got heavier, which added to his misery. But at least the thunder and lightning had stopped. It was chilly, though. He could have done with a nice flying jacket, like the one Toni wore, rather than the flimsy thing he usually wore. It was better than nothing, he supposed.

The run-down area he'd followed Miss Dominique to gradually changed back to the slightly nicer part of town, and he started to recognise various landmarks he must have passed earlier. It was dark, but he didn't think he'd been out for longer than a few minutes. The stiffness was easing as he walked, and still he concentrated on putting one foot in front of the other.

Ideally he could do with getting some digs closer to the river. That way he'd have more chance of seeing Miss Dominique when she returned. Meanwhile, he might have to just keep coming back to this part of town, so he tried to commit the directions to memory.

By instinct, he made his way back to the hotel he shared with Bart and Toni. Who knew, everyone might be back there by now and they could all get cosy and friendly again – and he could get a bath while his wet clothes dried. And then he could get something nice and hot to eat. His mouth started to water at the thought of food. He hadn't realised how hungry he was and once he did, that contributed to the dizziness.

Everything looked quite normal back at the hotel, so he collected his key and made his way up.

He was surprised to be greeted by two burly guards and the hotel manager, and the guards were both pointing guns at him.

HONDO PITTS COULDN'T find Mister Conrad. So he too made his way home and let himself into his apartment.

Within minutes of letting himself into the courtyard, he went into the meat locker to get food for the alligators. He chose several large chunks of meat that had been dropped off by the butcher and tipped the bucket into the courtyard pool. He didn't spend time these days watching the alligators come to eat. That particular novelty had worn off long since.

He made his way up the stairs and let himself into his room. He was supposed to be going out, but he couldn't be bothered. He had plenty in to throw together a meal of sorts, and he just stripped off his wet things and threw himself onto the cushion-strewn sofa, pulling one of the blankets around himself for extra warmth.

As the day's stress leached out of his aching body he started to nod off.

But in his semi-awake state he realised that he wasn't alone. There was someone in the back room of his apartment...

IT WASN'T BART OR TONI. They'd made a run for it, grabbing anything of worth from the room as they went by. Then they'd found the back stairs and made their way out of the back door of the hotel. As most of the staff were out front, responding to the phony fire alarm, there was no one to stop or question them.

"What do we do now?" asked Toni. "We can't go back. Someone knows we're here and they don't like it."

"Who were those goons?" asked Bart, completely ignoring her original question.

"I don't know. I thought they were security and the hotel manager."

"But they had guns?" Toni nodded. "Nah. They didn't look like anyone from the hotel to me."

"Then who could they be?"

"No idea. But you're right. We can't go back there."

The rain at least had stopped now, but they could still hear the rumble of thunder in the background and there was a chill in the air.

"Did you grab everything?" asked Bart. He knew he had.

"Yes," said Toni, holding up the bulging carpet bag.

"Perhaps we could go back to the witch-doctor's?" he suggested. "Odette said her sister might put us up. What was her name?"

"The fruit lady? That's Veronique. And yes, she did say she normally doesn't but might do as it's us."

They wrapped themselves up against the weather and headed off into the night, off to Desmond and Odette's.

THE CELL WAS DIRTY, dark and cold. Conrad perched on the edge of the rock-hard camp bed with his elbows on his knees and his head in his hands. There was a tiny little window up in the air where he couldn't see out. But there was no glass in the window, just bars, and the wind howled through. A stub of a candle sat on the floor, a bucket in the corner.

This wasn't supposed to happen. This wasn't in the plan. And at this time of night there was no chance of Hondo Pitts coming to get him. If they were in the twenty-first century he'd be able to call him, but they weren't.

He resigned himself to a night locked away from everything and everyone. He'd assumed the three men were hoods or gangsters. But they'd brought him to the police station, so either they were in cahoots with the cops or they were actual real life police. Conrad didn't even know they had them in New Orleans in 1926, unless it was some kind of sheriff's department.

Anyway, the police station was a lot more desirable than a hood's den might have been, so he made the bed as comfortable as he could, wrapped the flimsy blanket around himself, and lay down to sleep.

There were noises elsewhere in the police station that would have normally given Conrad the creeps – scratching, whimpering – but he knew it was likely just other prisoners in the jail.

Outside he heard the rain start again over the noise of the wind, fat, heavy raindrops competing with the howling gale. The thunder and lightning had stopped, but there was still an electrical storm happening not far away. He could hear it bubbling and spitting in the distance.

Another prisoner started to snore and a guard jangled some keys. But whether it was the knock on his head or a busy day, Conrad was very tired and didn't have any trouble going to sleep.

Which was why he was annoyed to be woken only a few short hours later by someone unlocking the gate to his cell very loudly.

He squinted into the bright light and shot upright.

"Come on. Let's get you out of here."

Chapter 18

AS USUAL, TONI AND Bart received a very warm welcome at Desmond and Odette's. The children were pleased to see them as well, and once again they had fresh coffee made for them as they sat on the sumptuous, plump cushions.

Such lovely, unassuming people who welcomed the brother and sister into their home.

Toni asked how their preparations were going for Mardi Gras. "And did you finish your outfit?" she asked Desmond.

His face split into a beaming, white smile and he wiggled a finger, saying, "Yes I did but you can't see it yet."

"Aww, you're such a spoilsport," teased Toni.

"Will you still be here for Mardi Gras?" asked Odette.

"It's starting to look like a possibility," agreed Bart.

"Then we will have to sort out some clothes for you to wear."

"How exciting," said Toni.

When they were finished, Odette told them how to find her sister Veronique's house.

"She'll be surprised to see you at this time of night," she said.

"I can go with them," said Gideon.

"Me too," said Esme."

Their parents exchanged glances, but agreed that the children could accompany them.

"It's not far," said Odette.

"Come straight back," said Desmond. "I'll keep watch for you, so get back before it gets really late."

Bart looked at the sky. It already looked really late to him.

"We'll be all right," said Toni.

"No," said Odette. "The children want to go and my sister will be happy to see them."

She went to the kitchen and got a package and gave it to Esme. "Give that to your aunt for me," she said.

Bart felt awkward. He didn't know what to say to a couple of children, and strangers at that really. So he just kept awkwardly quiet instead.

Toni was different. She always knew what to ask, and the three of them chattered away, about what their favourite lessons were in school, what their favourite games were, who their friends were, what they were doing for Mardi Gras.

Within a very short time they stopped and Esme pointed at another brightly painted front door.

"This is my aunt's house," she said.

Gideon went on ahead, pushed the door open and shouted a greeting to Veronique the fruit lady, who was surprised to see them but delighted that the children were there.

"Come in, come in," she said to them. "Who are your friends?"

"Don't you recognise them?" giggled the girl.

Veronique squinted at them both in the dim light, and they politely smiled back at her.

"Perhaps you'd recognise us better if we were covered in blood," said Toni at last.

There was another split second and the big fruit lady burst into a big deep-throated chortle.

"You look much better now," she said at last. "And your clothes are... are..."

"They belong to your sister," said Toni, holding up the bundle in her hand. "These are ours. Odette laundered them for us. We just prefer to explore the town in the ones she loaned to us."

"Well, they suit you both very well. Come on in and tell me what I can do for you."

She led them through a home that would, in later decades, be described as bohemian, but most of the houses and apartments here seemed to look like that.

"We need a room for the night," said Bart. "Odette said you used to let rooms out but didn't anymore, but you might let us stay."

"We can't stay," said Gideon, reminding his sister that they were supposed to go straight back."

"But Mama asked me to give you this," said Esme, holding out the package.

"Off you go, then, said Veronique to the children, seeing them safely out and along the road again for as long as she could, knowing full well that her brother-in-law would be watching for them as soon as they rounded the end of the street.

Once the door was closed again behind them, Veronique waddled back to the sitting room and addressed her guests.

"I don't let out rooms anymore," she agreed, "but if my sister sent you, you're very welcome."

"We can pay–" said Bart, realising as soon as he said it that he may be insulting the woman.

"I don't want your money," said Veronique. "But you're very welcome," she repeated. "Come on, I have a room ready, it just might need airing. When you've settled in you can tell me what's been happening to the two of you over the past few days."

THE ROOM WAS SMALL and dark but adequate, with two beds pushed apart and separated with a wooden chest. There was a tallboy for their clothes and a single chair, also wooden. All the wood was painted in different primary colours – the chest yellow, the tallboy red, the bedsteads blue. The floor was boards left rough, the walls were rough plaster, painted white. There were colourful curtains at the window, which Veronique had opened for them to let in some air. It was chilly and damp, though, with the storm outside, so they didn't think the window would be open for long but pulled back the covers on the beds to air them a little anyway.

When they'd hung their clothes in the closet and stashed their things, they returned to their hostess who had made fresh coffee for them all.

Toni thought that with all of this coffee they'd struggle to sleep, but it tasted rich and warm and comforting anyway. She wished they'd come to Veronique first and she briefly wondered where Conrad would be tonight if their room was still a mess.

Veronique inspected Toni's head wound and applied fresh dressings for her while they chatted. She asked if they would still be here for Mardi Gras.

"It's looking very likely," said Bart, for the second time that evening.

"I expect my sister has offered you an outfit each, then?"

They obviously knew each other very well.

She gave them some supper and they finally turned-in just as the storm outside was quieting down too. They both slept incredibly well and incredibly safely.

THE NEXT MORNING THEY enjoyed a breakfast of fruit and bread with milk. Veronique had work to do and so did they. But she said they were welcome to use the house while she was gone.

Toni and Bart did the only thing they thought they could do, under the circumstances. They made their way back to the cemetery so that they could have another go at the Harley and stow their belongings in the side-car.

"Did you see Veronique's radio?" asked Bart.

"No I didn't," replied Toni. "But you can't steal that. Or cannibalise it."

"Why not?"

"We can't steal from someone who's shown us such hospitality!"

"No, of course not. But we might be able to *borrow* it..."

"And what if it does the trick? Or if we need to break it to pieces before it can work? Will we be just *borrowing* it then?"

"Well, no. But at least we'd know if it worked or not."

"Hmm." Toni didn't like the idea but maybe he had a point.

"I don't mind so long as you put it back exactly as you found it."

When they retrieved the bike, they doubled back to help themselves to Veronique's radio. It was quite portable, but as they'd motorcycled back to her house they didn't have to carry the radio very far anyway. And they were able to park in her back yard and work there where no one could see them, and still have the warmth and shelter of the house if they needed it.

Toni watched as Bart fetched the radio and dismantled it on the kitchen table. He very carefully placed each of the components in a safe and logical place, so he could put it all together again quickly if necessary.

Before long all of the radio innards were spread across the table-top and Bart was scratching his head.

"Okay, Einstein," said his sister. "What now?"

"Now I have to go and dismantle the time-travel mechanism on the bike, see what works best. Do we still have those cogs you pinched from Conrad?"

She nodded and went to the side-car to get them from the bundle of their belongings grabbed from the hotel.

Toni added the cogs to the collection on the table, but put them a little to the side to differentiate them from the other gubbings.

Bart scratched his head again and then launched himself at the motorbike, lifting the seat and disappearing beneath the fairing. He was happy enough, tinkering away. But he needed to get the time machine fixed if they were to get home.

Toni watched him scurry backwards and forwards between the motorbike and the kitchen table, taking things, putting them back, sometimes adding to them. Then he suddenly started to put the radio back together and tidy away after himself.

"Have you done it?" asked Toni.

"I think so," he replied.

"That's good. How can we test it?"

"We'll have to test it when we're ready to go. I think we'll only get one pop at it."

"And what about the artefacts? Do we still need to find those?"

"I think so. We may never be able to return to this exact time, so we need to reap what we can and then get out of here."

"And Conrad?"

"What about Conrad?"

"Whatever he's done, we can't leave him here."

"He found his own way here. I'm sure he can find his own way back again."

Bart returned the radio to the shelf where he'd found it and they were just leaving when the radio burst into life.

"Did you switch it on?" asked Toni.

"Nope."

"Then it must be the boss."

The two of them went and sat in front of the radio.

"(Crackle, crackle,)" it said, so Bart thumped it on the side. "Ouch!"

"Sorry!"

"Now listen very... (crackle, crackle,)" said the radio.

Chapter 19

"HOW DID YOU KNOW WHERE to find me?" Conrad had asked when Hondo turned up to rescue him the night before.

The bead-seller indicated a small boy lurking in the shadows.

"I had him follow the girl but when she spotted him he ran off. He came back later and reported to me that he'd found you lying face down in the mud not far from Miss Dominique's neighbourhood. By the time we got there to help you, you were already on your way back to the hotel. I had some business to attend to so the boy followed you to the hotel and kept watch. By the time I got there, you'd been arrested and he didn't know what to do. So he waited for me to turn up and when I did we both headed to the jail.

"It took some persuading, and some cash – you might want to pay me back some of that – but eventually they let us see you. And you know the rest."

"He's a good boy," said Conrad, nodding in the boy's direction.

"You might want to give him a little something too."

Conrad nodded.

He'd spent the night on Hondo Pitts' couch, considerably more comfortable than he'd thought his night was going to be. And warmer. And there was hot coffee too. And hygienic sanitary conditions.

"Do you know where Toni and Bart went?"

"No," said Hondo. "When I got there earlier, the place was empty. A mess, but empty. There had just been a fire alarm, a false alarm. I think they may have sneaked out the back way."

Conrad pointed to the boy. "He doesn't know where they are either?"

"Can speak for m'self," said the boy.

"Course you can," agreed Conrad.

"Ask me, then."

Conrad shrugged, and said: "Do you know where they are?"

The boy shook his head and Conrad sighed.

"But I can find out," said the boy, and Conrad brightened.

"You do that," he said.

THE RADIO MESSAGE WAS their best yet, but it was still very crackly. Bart and Toni hoped that every message from now on would be that good, but if they were honest, they realised that the boss was starting to run out of channels. He'd used almost every available one now and they weren't sure if he could use them again. They'd got gradually better. All they needed now was a newspaper telling them exactly what they had to find, where to find it and what to do with it. But, of course, life wasn't that simple.

"So we have to find our own amulet," said Bart.

"Check," said Toni.

"And we have to get Conrad's amulet."

"Check."

"We have to keep them both apart and take them back to the future and put them in safe-keeping."

"Check."

"Then we have to find a single crystal and two cogs, and we have to connect them with three valves from a radio."

"Check."

"Which means we have to cannibalise a radio..."

"That's right."

As the only working radio they'd found so far belonged to Veronique, neither of them felt very happy about that particular part.

"And once the connection is made, we'll be on our way back."

"Check."

"But we already have one amulet," said Bart.

"We do," agreed Toni.

"Do you think it matter's which one is which?"

"What do you mean?"

"Well, do you think it matters if we already have Conrad's or if we already have our own?"

"I don't know, but I'm pretty sure it's Conrad's that we have. I'm sure he would have given it to the bead-seller for safe-keeping once he got here."

"But what if there are three amulets?" mused Bart. "We can't take the wrong one in case it interferes with history."

"Well, the boss said that one of the amulets is in a back room, didn't he?" Bart nodded. "And we found Hondo Pitts' amulet in a back room."

"So that means it's one of the right ones?"

"Perhaps."

"He said the other amulet was somewhere else, that it had only just arrived in the city," said Bart.

"So that must have been on the boat," agreed Toni. "It's the only thing that's also just arrived in the city."

"What did he say about it already being here?" asked Bart.

"He said it was hidden where we were supposed to find it in 1942 much later than now but that this might be a good time to get it before then anyway."

Well, it made sense to Toni, despite a puzzled look from Bart.

"If we can't find it," he said, at last, "then we'll just have to go back without it and come back again to the right date."

"That could be expensive, though. If we can find it now, before it gets hidden in its first hiding place, then we could save time and money."

Bart rubbed his chin while he thought of a solution.

"I bet it just gets shoved in a cupboard and then gets moved when the owner moves to a new part of town," he said. "The new part of town that hasn't been built yet."

"But why would anyone want to move to a different part of town?" asked Toni.

Bart shrugged his shoulders. "Anything. Work. Betterment. Marriage. Perhaps it's an old people's home or some other kind of sanatorium."

"In the 1940s?" asked Toni. "I'd bet it's a loony bin."

"God, I wish we had Google," said Bart.

"I bet Conrad checked Google before he came too," said Toni.

"So he'd know where to find this extra amulet, not knowing we already have the other one?"

Brother and sister looked at each other and exchanged a knowing glance. They both knew what the other was thinking. But it was Toni who voiced it.

"Then we need to find out where Conrad got to and follow him."

"Or insist on tagging along with him wherever he goes. He won't know we already have the other amulet."

"Okay," said Toni, counting things off on her hands. "We have one amulet. We're going to follow Conrad to find the other amulet – unless we run out of time. We know where there are some radio valves if we can't find another radio. We have the cogs. What we don't have is the crystal."

Silence.

"Hmm," said Bart at last. "Pity the boss didn't tell us where to find that before he got cut off."

"Or what it looks like," agreed Toni.

"It could be anywhere," mused Bart.

"And it could be anything," said Toni.

It was time for dinner as Bart's belly was rumbling and he hated to be hungry.

"Do you think Veronique will be back by noon?" he asked his sister.

"I don't know, but I think if she does and we're still here, we might be over-staying our welcome a bit. We can stay here for at least another night, but then we need to be going home."

"Yes," said Bart. "We have just under twenty-four hours to find this crystal, another radio if we can, and get the time machine working."

"And, of course," said Toni, "It's Mardi Gras tomorrow. The town is going to be busy."

"Mega-busy," agreed her brother.

And off they went in search of first food and then Conrad.

Chapter 20

ON THE OTHER SIDE OF town, Conrad and Hondo were having a similar conversation – just apart from the bit about time travel and messages from the future.

"Does she show any sign of being a bit nuts?" asked Conrad.

"Who? Miss Halima? Not that I know of. But there is a rumour that she likes her opium and her booze–"

"Booze? Where does she get that from?" Conrad knew alcohol was prohibited in the United States during the 1920s.

"Black market I guess," shrugged Pitts.

"And does she have a temper when she's, er, drunk or stoned?"

"Oh yeah. She's known for it."

Ah, thought Conrad. That would be it. In their ignorance, the powers that be would probably put her away in the loony bin when really, if it was the twenty-first century, they'd put her in rehab. In these olden days, being black wouldn't help her either.

"Have there been any complaints so far?" he asked.

"Not that I've noticed," replied Pitts.

He needed to get to her now, before they put her away, and retrieve the other amulet from her. He couldn't buy it or anything as that might change the course of history. But he wished he could warn her what would happen if she didn't give up her vices.

HALIMA DOMINIQUE WAS brought up in the slums of old New Orleans when she was spotted by a talent scout from the showboat. All she'd been doing was playing in the yard with her old gollywog, singing to it, when a total stranger overheard her. Of course, she didn't have such a glamorous name in those days. The name Halima Dominique was given to her to make her seem more exotic so that people would pay more money to see her.

Fame didn't suit her very well, though, and it was her manager who got her onto the dope in the first place, and then into the whiskey. It helped her to sleep, or it helped her have the courage to perform, or it kept her awake. Whatever she needed, opium and whiskey did the trick. But Halima Dominique wanted to be normal, get married, have children, and she never knew whether the men who showed an interest in her did so for her or because of who she was. And, eventually, by 1926, she was totally dependent on the drugs and the booze.

It was during Mardi Gras of 1926 that Halima was kidnapped. But she was able to hide her most treasured possessions in a secret compartment hidden under the house.

Several years later, when she was allowed home again, she retrieved her goods and took them to a totally new part of town. But she was still a very sick and lonely woman, hooked now on quaaludes and other drugs of the day, and she was to be locked up again in a new mental institution in a new part of town, and this time she was given electric shock treatment.

She'd been allowed to take her personal belongings with her this time and while she never really opened the old jewellery box and examined its contents, she still kept it close to her, hidden beneath the floorboards in her hospital room until the day she died.

Toni and Bart were supposed to go back to the mental hospital in 1948. But to beat them to it, Conrad had instead travelled back to 1926 and hoped to find the treasure stash before the house became inhabited again by a new family. What he hadn't reckoned on was Toni and Bart landing there too. He just wanted to delay their arrival at the hospital to give him chance to stop the amulet being moved there anyway. But he'd obviously fixed their time machine good and proper.

The amulets were from the old voodoo and each apparently had a curse on them that could only be broken if they were kept separated. But legend had it that once the amulets were reunited, the owner would be miraculously showered with wealth so vast he'd never have to work again.

Conrad longed for the day that he didn't have to work again, but until then, or if it wasn't possible, he just wanted the company. The company that should have by right gone to him but had instead skipped him and gone to his younger brother due to a fall-out with their father who no longer trusted his first-born.

But if he could get hold of both of those amulets together, then he wouldn't have to worry about the company ever again. Or his stupid little brother.

"Boss?" said Hondo Pitts, drawing him from his reverie. "You were miles away there, boss."

Chapter 21

LAST MINUTE PREPARATIONS were underway. Flags and banners were added to lamps and balconies not yet decorated, or those that had lost their decorations in the storm of the previous day. What little litter there was was swept away and extra bins – decorated of course – were put outside shops and bars. Stallholders set up their stalls, doing any last-minute carpentry or making any repairs following the storm. A bonfire on a bit of spare ground received its finishing touches, but other bits were added as people passed. People cleaned their windows at the front of houses and shops, or they polished their steps to within an inch of their shine, or they washed down any paintwork or removed any loose flakes. Some were even painting or repairing the brickwork or the stucco.

Men, women and children scurried from door to door, their piles of purchases getting taller. Roads, footpaths and gutters were swept, broken glass was replaced. It was a bustle of activity.

"It'll be worse tomorrow," said Bart.

"But tomorrow there will be bright outfits, shiny brass bands, beautiful dancers. No one will worry how their house looks tomorrow."

They passed a furniture shop that had radios for sale, but they were too expensive or too big or too old-fashioned to be of any use to them. And so they pressed on regardless towards the cemetery where Conrad had left the car, hoping it would still be there. The car was as good a place as anywhere they might find Conrad.

But there was no sign of him or the bead-seller or of the boy Toni had seen the other day.

"Shall we try the port?" asked Bart.

"May as well," shrugged Toni.

The port was as busy as the town with the same kind of activity going on. Two men were arranging folding chairs in rows facing the showboat.

"Looks like they might be having an open-air performance," commented Toni.

The ensemble could be seen boarding the boat and making their way to their various cabins to make final preparations for tomorrow's show. Children got in the way playing marbles and jackstones on the floor, but every time someone kicked them or complained, they just laughed, made a rude gesture with their hands, and moved on. One small group of children, all girls, hung around the end of the gangplank, hoping to catch the eye of their favourite dancer, singer or actor. Most of the performers humoured them.

A white man wandered around with a large camera on a tripod across his shoulder and a large flash gun in his hand. They watched him set up in a corner, sheltered from the weather by two walls of the port buildings. He started to offer his service for a small fee. He kept a small notebook and pencil to jot down their names and addresses, and he had a suitcase with props of feather boas and various hats.

Corn dog and hamburger sellers began to arrive, securing the best spot for selling their wares.

Bart at first eyed up the photographer's flash gun, no doubt wondering if the element inside might be of any use, but he was distracted by the smell of cooking burgers and Toni could swear she heard his mouth water.

Of Conrad and the bead-seller there was still no sign, but Toni did catch sight of someone that she did recognise, loitering around the ladies and gentlemen of the showboat.

She tugged at Bart's sleeve.

"There's that boy I saw following me," she said.

Bart looked to where she was pointing.

"Are you sure?"

"Yes. He was wearing the same clothes."

They hid behind the corn dog seller while they watched the boy watching the folk arriving on and leaving the boat. He didn't seem to be interested in anything else happening on the riverbank, just who was coming and going on the boat. And he wasn't particularly watching the men either.

"He's only looking at the women," whispered Toni.

"Wait, he's seen something," said Bart, catching hold of her arm.

The boy ducked behind some barrels and his eyes watched someone leaving the boat, a woman, a pretty little thing dressed like a flapper beneath a long fur coat. Under her arm she carried a parcel wrapped in brown paper and tied with string. Her own eyes darted around the port, looking for someone, not seeing them, and she decided to walk into the town.

The boy followed at a safe distance.

So Toni and Bart followed him too, also at a safe distance.

They walked through the busy town to a much poorer section, where the houses grew more shabby and more dilapidated. There were not as many street decorations here, but there were not as many people either and the boy – and Toni and Bart – had to drop back further to avoid being seen.

The woman disappeared inside a small house on the edge of the town, and the boy hung around at the end of the street wondering whether or not to stay. Toni and Bart decided to stay for now, at least until either the boy or the woman made another move.

It was the boy who went first.

"What do we do now?" hissed Bart.

"You follow the boy, I'll watch the house."

Toni positioned herself against another house, in the lee of the overhanging roof, with her back to the wall.

"Okay," said Bart, heading off after the boy.

Toni stayed in her relatively sheltered position but she did feel a chill. She pulled her leather jacket around her more tightly, zipped it up to the top, held onto her thumbs – where she'd been told once there was a pulse that would keep her warmer – and thrust her hands into the fleece-lined pockets. She pushed her chin inside her jacket so that her hot breath warmed her through too.

When there was no sign of life from the house the woman had gone into, Toni crept closer and did a full circuit of the building. Through a back window she could see the woman moving around.

The woman unwrapped the brown paper parcel. Inside was a bejewelled hip-flask. The woman unscrewed the cap and took a deep drink, the sour liquid making her grimace but then clearly hitting the spot. Toni looked at her watch. It wasn't even noon yet.

The first thing to occur to Toni was that she was a lush. The second thing to occur was that this was 1926. Prohibition was in place. Not only was this woman drinking liquor at an unusually early hour, but she was also breaking the law.

As the woman moved around the house, from room to room, Toni carefully followed on the outside. And through the other window at the back she was startled to see a hookah pipe smoking and bubbling away.

The woman was a junkie! Or someone in the house was.

Not wanting to be seen by anyone, Toni moved away from the house and sat on a small wall beneath a tree, from where she could watch the woman's front door quite safely from a distance and not be seen quite so easily.

As she sat and mulled, something else occurred to Toni while she waited. In fact, it struck her so suddenly and so strongly she could almost see the light bulb above her head flash on brightly.

Without her big fur coat, Toni could see the woman's dress. And around her neck, on a leather thong, was an amulet. The double of the one they already had.

Toni could hardly wait to tell Bart.

BART KEPT GOOD PACE with the boy as they retraced their steps through the town. He'd stayed a fair distance behind and every time the boy stopped, Bart walked in a different direction, averting his face.

Very soon he started to recognise his surroundings and he didn't need to follow the lad up the alley between the houses. The boy was going to the bead-seller's house. So Bart was able to hang around in the square rather than follow the boy and draw unnecessary attention to himself. There was plenty to look at in the square as it too prepared for the fiesta of the following day. And it was so busy it was easy to mingle and not be noticed.

Before long the boy re-emerged from the alley, but this time he had Conrad and the bead-seller, Hondo Pitts, in tow. The two men must have been taken by surprise as they were both still doing up their coats. And Conrad tugged down his hat. The group quickly made their way back through the town, the boy running ahead, the adults trying to keep up with him without drawing too much attention to themselves. And several feet behind them trailed Bart, also trying not to draw attention to himself.

The group in front drew attention to themselves in another way, however, by shoving and pushing people out of the way. If anyone got in front of them, either by accident or a hawker wanting to sell them something, they just ignored them. If anyone stumbled or just plain got in the way, they forced their way through. At one point they even knocked a woman's wares all across the road and didn't even bat an eyelid, let alone say sorry or offer to help.

By the time they reached the woman's house in the shabby part of town, Bart started to worry about whether or not they'd see Toni. He needn't have worried, though. When he got there himself, there was no sign of her.

Chapter 22

BART DIDN'T KNOW WHETHER to panic and show himself, or hang back and keep quiet.

Conrad and Hondo Pitts followed the boy right up to the front door of the house. Conrad knocked on the door. When there was no answer he knocked again, this time much louder. There was still no answer and he started to circle the house and peer in at the windows. As far as Bart could see, the curtains or blinds were all drawn. But still Conrad cupped his hand to block out the light as he tried to see through.

Bart watched as Hondo Pitts and the boy did the exact same thing, following and copying Conrad like sheep.

But no. There was no sign of life from the house.

He kept his distance and watched as Conrad tried the door handle. The handle gave and the men and the boy were able to simply walk in.

Bart lingered around outside and waited for them to complete their inspection. When they came out, they huddled together to obviously discuss whatever situation they thought was going down. Then they made their way back to the town, resigned to their journey being a waste of time.

He waited until they were well and truly out of sight before he too ventured into the house. He wanted to see if there were signs of a struggle or, worse, any blood.

The house, and indeed the whole of this neighbourhood, seemed to be a bit of a throwback to grander times that had been allowed to grow shabby and unmaintained over the years. As if the money that was one here had moved on elsewhere in the city. The houses were quite elaborate but small affairs, perhaps struggling for the grandeur of bigger mansions that the rich had lived in.

The street consisted of small wooden houses that were either built as single dwellings or two dwellings stuck together, like a semi. This house, a pair, used to be painted white, but a lot of the paint had peeled. Both houses were long and narrow, each with an individual flight of five stone steps leading up to a private front door, one at either edge of the house. Next to the door was a floor-to-ceiling ten-pained sash.

The house next door had painted wooden louvred shutters over its front door and front window, both closed. But the house he was looking at was just the bare door and window.

Five wooden pillars held the porch roof up across the whole front of the property, and a little wooden frieze ran around the top. There were curtains up at the window and a blind up at the door. Gold plated numbers above the door in the pane of glass had peeled away too, but these houses were definitely up in the 2,000s.

A wrought-iron fence flanked the steps and ran along the front of the terrace, separating it from the street to give it some privacy. Two in-built troughs overflowed with dead greenery, parched to death in the summer but starting to come back after the recent storms.

The next-door neighbour had a nice potted palm outside the front of their house, but this one had a broken pot on its side, the contents long spilled out.

He knew the door was open as he'd just watched Conrad let himself in, so Bart pushed the door handle and did the same.

The house was long and thin, with one room leading into another and then that one leading into another. He could see right through to the back door, and he wondered if this was what they called shotgun houses in New Orleans. If it was, he could see why someone would be able to shoot from one end of the house to another without hindrance.

This first room was the living room, from what he could gather. But, like the other homes he'd seen in the town, it was, again, very bohemian in its style with drapes and curtains and wall hangings all over the place, some separating the rooms where a door would normally be. There was a divan-style settee built-in to the recess next to the kitchenette, and a small, scrubbed dining table with two chairs tucked under was pushed up against the kitchen counter. There were floorboards covered with rugs in this room, but in the kitchen area was a tile-effect vinyl-type floor covering.

A hubble-bubble pipe sat on a side table, still smoking from whatever was in it. Next to it was a bejewelled hip-flask now empty but smelling strongly of absinthe. Bart pocketed the hip-flask. It fitted quite snugly against his hip. Then he placed it back on the side table where it belonged. Next to the pipe was a table-top radio, and he resisted an urge to pick that up too.

There hadn't been a struggle here, but it did look a bit abandoned. The rugs were thread-bare, the floorboards and the lino in the kitchen badly scuffed.

Bart walked slowly past the kitchen, where pots and pans and cups and plates were piled in and around a small sink area. The next room was a sitting room. Aside from a fireplace with a rocking chair in front of it there was also an upright piano in this room. That was interesting, but then he supposed that a musical town like New Orleans would have lots of musical instruments tucked away.

Again, the floor here was boards, but a larger, newer rug sat on the floor.

The walls were wood panelling with a large but dirty mirror over the empty fireplace and other small works of art in various spaces.

The next room was kitted out as a bedroom with just a camp-style bed pushed beneath the single window, a small wooden tallboy, and a single chair. The last room was a bigger bedroom that had a double bed with a wrought-iron bedstead and a patchwork quilt across it. The bed hadn't been made and there were clothes strewn about the room. But here there was also a large chest of drawers, a small writing desk, a bedside table, two wooden chairs – one another rocker – and lino again on the floor with a brightly coloured rug over the top.

The door here led out to a back yard with a very small entry that took him back to the street. He looked up and down at the nicely kept but old and shabby homes, all of them semis with a single tiny window in the roof space. He assumed this was attic space and maybe the house on the left had the back of the attic and the house on the right had the front attic. Some had wooden stairs with banisters leading up to the front doors, others were, like this one, stone.

Bart went back inside the house. He was sorely tempted to start taking the radio to bits, but he resisted, sat on the rocker in the middle sitting room and waited.

CONRAD AND HONDO AND the boy made their way back to Hondo's place.

"I've been meaning to ask," said Conrad, as they passed the alligator pit at the front of the complex, "why the, er, pets?"

Hondo Pitts went into the downstairs storeroom and got the creatures some meat. The three of them watched as four alligators came to feast on the offering.

"That's my main business," said Hondo. Shoes, boots and ladies' pocketbooks. They also make belts, watch bands and wallets."

"They don't seem to have a lot of room," said Conrad.

Hondo laughed. "Come on, I'll show you." He led them out of the yard, down the alley, around the buildings and into what looked like a smallholding, perhaps an acre or so, with nothing but delta on the other side of a fence. He hadn't realised these houses were on the edge of town.

The small area was landscaped like a water park, but basking alligators could be seen on some of the little islands within the manmade ponds.

"The ponds in the yard are connected to the delta underground. They can get into the rivers from here, and they hunt and swim and wander. But if they know they're being fed, they keep coming back. And when they're close enough, we can shoot them. We sell the meat too. And the teeth for jewellery. I've even made some necklaces out of them myself. Do you want one?"

Conrad shuddered at the thought, but didn't like to appear rude or ungrateful, so he changed the subject.

"And you make money from that?"

"Enough. It was the tooth necklaces that got me into the beads. You can only sell so many alligator-tooth necklaces or bracelets, but you can sell lots of glass beads to lots of people. Between the two businesses, I live well enough."

They went back to Hondo's apartment and he told the boy to scoot.

"See if you can find out anything about Miss Dominique and come back to let us know, okay?"

The boy nodded and ran off.

Conrad and Hondo made their way upstairs again where Pitts rustled up something for them to eat and a drink of coffee. And he told Conrad more about the alligator business and how it was seasonal.

They got back onto the subject of Halima Dominique and Toni and Bart again, wondering what had happened to them all over the past day or so as they'd lost contact since the hotel room was raided.

"Do you still have the amulet?" asked Conrad.

"Of course I do," said Hondo, going into his back room and coming back with his little treasure pot.

But when he opened it and looked in, his face dropped.

"It's gone," he said.

Chapter 23

BART LISTENED TO THE ticking of the clock on the mantelpiece. It was very relaxing, hypnotising almost. And it was while he was daydreaming that another thought occurred to him.

A clock.

They already had the cogs from Conrad's stash in the car and he knew they could do with some valves from a radio. But a clockwork mechanism? That could only be useful too. His hands itched as he resisted helping himself, and he let the ticking of the clock lull him into a doze.

The clock struck one o'clock and Bart awoke with a start. But it wasn't just the chime that had woken him. There was someone in the house.

He stood up and crept to the curtain that separated the middle room from the front room, and heaved an audible sigh of relief.

"Toni!" he said. "Where have you been?"

"I was following our little lush from here."

"Did she go out?"

"No. Two men came and got her. She was scared stiff when she saw them, but she went without a fight."

"What did they look like?"

"They were both big, white, youngish. They wore heavy coats and large hats that shaded their faces. But I heard some of what they had to say."

"Was it interesting?"

"Well, not to me. But I don't think she'll be coming back here."

"Ever?" Toni shook her head. "Why not?"

"I think she was a runaway slave–"

"Slave? But slavery was abolished... over a hundred years ago..."

"Actually, it was only sixty years ago here – we're in 1926, remember. And I think the deep south held onto their servants a while longer anyway. In fact, I'm sure there are some here that still do."

"What made you think she was a runaway?"

"Just that they shouted at her that she'd led them a merry dance and how changing her name hadn't helped. That she shouldn't have joined the showboat if she hadn't wanted to be found. They'd been watching her for a few days, even stopped someone else stalking her only a day or so ago, while they checked who she was and where she came from. Then they frog-marched her out of the house without letting her collect any of her things."

"Why do you think she won't be back?"

"Because they took her to a big house on the outskirts of town and locked her in the basement, told her she'd have to stay there until she realised what was good for her. And then, if the boss'm allowed it, she'd be let back into the kitchen to resume her duties."

"Poor cow," said Bart.

"Poor junkie too," said Toni. "The way she was puffing on that pipe thing and swigging from that hip flask, she's going to go into cold turkey before the end of tomorrow."

"Well, that might not do her very much harm, if she is an addict."

"Yes, but it might also kill her. Or, if she gets nasty, she might kill someone."

"Sounds like she'll have to escape first."

Bart was very happy to see his sister safe and well, but he was also keen to know what she thought about the woman's things.

"If she isn't coming back, she might not need her stuff."

"What stuff were you thinking of?"

"There's a clock in the middle room," he indicated over his shoulder with his thumb. "Then there's this here radio," he pointed at the side table. "And that hip flask might come in handy too."

"What could you want with a hip flask?"

"It's encrusted with gems. Ideally we could do with a crystal, but one of those gemstones might be good enough – if they're real. Or even if they're not. One of them just might be the right size, shape and consistency."

"Hmm," said Toni, "I see your reasoning."

He waited a moment to see if he would get his sister's blessing, but she was deliberately not going to give it.

"Tone."

"What?" she smirked, knowing full well what he wanted.

"If she's not coming back..."

"Yes...?"

"Couldn't we... borrow her radio?"

"And her clock? And her hip flask?"

"Well, yes, now you come to mention them."

"But we're not going to lug them across town, are we?"

"No," replied Bart. "In fact, if she's not coming back, I don't see why we can't stay here tonight. There's food and coffee and a kind of squash drink in the pantry in the kitchen."

"No fridge?"

"No fridge."

"Okay, I'll go for a wander while you spread out on that kitchen table."

"Actually," said Bart, "it might be worth going to get the bike too."

"Is it not best hidden?"

"There's a yard out back and I need the time machine anyway, so I can work on it."

"Come on, then, let's go and get the bike."

"Actually..." said Bart.

"What...?"

"You may as well stay here, make sure no one comes back."

"We're already taking a punt on her living here on her own," said Toni.

"Only one person lives here," said Bart. "I've seen the rest of the house."

"And if she was an escaped servant, it might be that she was squatting anyway."

"Or it belongs to her family."

They had no way of knowing. But Toni agreed to stay behind and keep watch while he went for the bike.

"But while you're gone," she added, "get us some bread and fruit and cream and stuff."

CONRAD WAS FURIOUS. The boy ran off while Hondo Pitts stood there, the open box in his hand.

"Why don't you people lock your doors?" blustered Conrad, starting to turn purple.

"There's not usually any need," replied Hondo. "Until you lot arrived."

"When was the last time you checked it?" asked Conrad.

"The day you gave it to me."

"But that was three days ago."

"And?"

"Well, anyone could have been in here since then."

"Like who?"

"Like bloody Miss Twinkle-toes and Mister Butter-wouldn't-melt."

Hondo Pitts had no idea what he was talking about.

"Never mind," said Conrad. "So much for them bloody crocodiles too."

"Alligators," said Hondo, helpfully.

"What?"

"We have alligators."

"Oh, shut up!"

"Okay, boss."

"Has that box been anywhere else?" asked Conrad.

Keeping his lips firmly sealed and blowing his cheeks out, Hondo shook his head.

"Then they must have been here. And I bet they took something from the car."

Hondo Pitts watched as the truth of that last throwaway statement hit home.

"I bet she did," repeated Conrad, jumping up and grabbing his hat and jacket.

Hondo Pitts followed him out of the apartment, along the alley and out into the town again, half running to keep up with the other man's long gait – and aggressive speed. As he ran, he did up his jacket and pulled his hat down tighter on his head.

When they got to the cemetery, there was another funeral in progress, so they had to slow down, partly to show respect, but also because they couldn't get through. Conrad grew more and more frustrated until he was able to reach his precious motor car. He even forgot to check that no one was paying too much attention as he rolled the stone out of the way.

Hondo waited outside the tomb. It was tight enough in there with a motor car parked up without him jostling for room with Conrad too. He could hear the banging and clattering coming from inside as Conrad opened the car, lifted the loose floorboard, and retrieved his stash box.

There was silence, a few expletives, and Hondo Pitts guessed that something had indeed disappeared from the boss's precious chest.

As he emerged from the mausoleum, Conrad cursed some more.

"What did she take, boss?" asked Hondo, bravely.

Conrad shook his head and stormed out of the cemetery. All Pitts could do was keep up.

As they passed the other cemetery, Conrad saw something else to make his blood boil and Hondo Pitts heard an almighty roar.

Bart was wearing his goggles so Hondo wasn't sure it was him. Conrad recognised him straight away, though. Or he recognised the motorbike and side-car he was driving. Hondo thought it was quite a nice, tidy piece of kit, but he felt a cuff around the earhole as his boss reminded him he wasn't here to admire the opposition's transport.

"But boss, it's a new motorbike. I've not seen one of those before."

"And you might not see one again if you don't keep up."

There was no way they would catch Bart on foot, and they didn't have time to go back and get the car. They had no choice but to let him go. At least they knew now that he was still alive, still in town, and probably so was his sister.

THE CLOCK ON THE MANTELPIECE chimed the quarter hour. Bart had been gone for well over an hour, almost two hours. Toni was starting to worry.

And she was hungry.

She needn't have worried as she heard the roar of the motorbike coming towards her. She hoped he had some food.

Her brother bounced into the house, a paper bag filled with groceries under one arm and a newspaper under the other.

He placed the bag down on the kitchen counter and opened the newspaper on the kitchen table.

"Looks like the boss has been in contact with us again," he said, pointing to the leader article on page three.

Chapter 24

THE ARTICLE TOOK UP about a quarter of a page of the broadsheet newspaper. There was a big, smiling picture of the boss, sitting sideways on a bench with one of his leather-booted legs bent up onto the bench. He was wearing suede trousers and a tweed jacket, and looked as though he were posing for a men's lifestyle magazine photo-shoot.

"Heck, It's good to see him," said Bart.

"What does he say?" asked Toni, trying to read over her brother's shoulder.

Bart started to read the story aloud to her. "It's in code," he said.

"That's okay," replied his sister taking out a notepad and pen. She knew the cypher.

In order to fix the time machine, they needed a clock mechanism, a crystal, two radio valves, a radio antenna, the filament from inside a Tungsten light-bulb, some calcium carbonate, magnesium wire, a firing pin and enough electricity to cause the light-bulb to flash.

Everything they needed could be found in their current surroundings.

However, in order to fix the time momentum thing they went back for, they had to be present at the Mardi Gras when an actress called Halima Dominique would be arrested and locked up so that her house remained intact until her release twenty-two years later. The risk was that someone would either help her escape or get her killed, and that would ruin everything and cause the company to start to fade.

There followed a detailed description of Miss Halima Dominique, who was apparently addicted to alcohol and to drugs.

"That sounds like our landlady," said Bart.

"I didn't realise she was an actress," said Toni. "I can't see her hogging the limelight at all."

"But I bet she came in on the showboat," said Bart.

"And that's what Conrad was waiting for," agreed Toni.

"No wonder he was furious when the boat was late."

Once Miss Dominique had been taken into custody it would be safe for them to fire up the machine and come home.

But they'd only get one shot at cranking the time machine fully. So they had to make sure they had all of the components, or similar, before even attempting to reboot.

They didn't need to worry about the amulet at this stage, unless they stumbled upon it anyway. They were to concentrate on foiling this particular time sabotage and get back home. They could always go again to get the artefact.

According to the weather forecast, which was immediately below the article, there was to be another thunderstorm tomorrow afternoon.

Toni looked at Bart, a question on her face.

"What?"

"She's already been locked up."

"Then we need to help her escape."

"But she seems like such a sweet, gentle thing."

"We can't meddle," he reminded her.

"No," she sighed. "But where will we find all of that stuff?"

Bart glanced down the list again.

"We already have a clock mechanism and a radio," he said. "Looks like those cogs are useless."

"Unless he took them out of our time machine and they need to go back."

"Mm," said Bart. "That could work."

"What about the rest of it?"

"There was a photographer down by the riverside," he said. "He might have the calcium carbonate and the magnesium wire–"

"But what is that even?"

"Some photographers used it before the flashbulb was invented. Apparently, quite a few died."

"Can we get a Tungsten light-bulb from him too?"

"I doubt it, but I think I know where we might find one. You gave me the clue."

"What did I say?"

"You mentioned how our landlady might like the limelight..."

"And?"

"Where do you think that expression came from? It's what the footlights were made of." She still wasn't convinced. "The showboat? They'll have a stage. I bet they have footlights and spotlights too."

"Oh yeah," said Toni, feeling a little dim. She looked at the list over her brother's shoulder again. "We don't have a crystal or a firing pin, though. Or a radio antenna."

"The antenna will be easy. All we need is a piece of rod. But our landlady's hip flask is studded with gems. If we can't find a crystal in any of these heeby-jeeby voodoo shops, we might be able to use one of those stones. A firing pin we still have to find."

"But what about the electricity?"

"I think that's what the radio antenna is for." Toni's face may as well have turned into a giant question-mark when she looked at her brother again. "To conduct electricity. From the storm." Nope, still nothing. "Lightning. Lightning conductor. Electricity generation."

"Oh, that's clever," she said.

"Not really," he admitted. "It was in a computer game I played once, one of the first that came out." He cast about in his memory for the title. "I can't remember what it was called but they had a kite and they needed to generate electricity to power a Hoover, so they flew the kite in an electrical storm and conducted the power from a flash of lightning."

"Sounds like fun," said Toni. "I feel deprived now."

"Anyway," continued Bart. "We need to help our lady escape so that she can be at the Mardi Gras tomorrow. Do you remember where they took her?"

"Yes, but it's a long walk."

He jangled his bike keys in front of her face. "We have the Harley here now," he said.

They retrieved their goggles from the side-car, hopped on and off they went, to the big house on the outskirts of town where the two men had taken the woman who's house they'd borrowed. The bike was a bit too noisy to sneak up on anyone, though. So they had to park it in a tree-lined avenue and walk the rest of the way.

The house loomed up on them as they rounded a bend. It was set back from the main road but there was no wall around it, just shrubs and trees. There were lots of windows, so the chances of them being seen were quite high.

"Perhaps we need to come back in the dark," said Bart.

"I agree," said Toni.

They headed back to the bike and back to Miss Dominique's house.

CONRAD WAS HOPPING mad. His amulet had been stolen. His cogs had been stolen. What did they even need those for? He didn't understand why they'd take them when he needed them for his own time machine. He'd taken them out for security reasons, rather like an immobiliser on a car. If they weren't in place then no one could accidentally start the time machine. But without them, neither could he.

Without the amulet there was no reason to try and steal the other one. And even if they had the one, there was nothing to guarantee they had the other one too. Why would they? They didn't even know where to find it in this time zone. Their amulet was hidden away in a lunatic asylum that hadn't even been built yet, so it hadn't been moved there yet either.

He had no idea where Toni and Bart were or where they were staying. All he did know was that they hadn't been back to their hotel room and they'd cleared it out before leaving.

"Did they take anything else?" asked Hondo Pitts.

"I still have my coins, if that's what you mean," replied Conrad. "Don't worry, you'll get your wages."

"Do you want me to send the boy off after them, see if he can find them?" asked Pitts.

"May as well," said Conrad, losing his fire now.

"We can split up and look," suggested Pitts.

They still had a whole afternoon of daylight, so grudgingly, Conrad agreed.

"We'll meet up back at yours at six o'clock?" he suggested, all the wind knocked out of him but he had to go through the motions anyway. Hondo Pitts nodded and they split up.

All Conrad could do was stroll through the town asking people as they went if they'd seen a man and a woman who matched his description. But not many remembered a couple, although some remembered the man on his own.

Perhaps they'd split up too.

A stray dog wandered into his line of vision and he realised he hadn't really seen many animals, apart from those horses people were still using. The dog sat down in front of him and looked at him in an expectant manner, head cocked to once side, tongue lolling out making him look like he was laughing.

"What do you want?" grunted Conrad, and the dog cocked his head some more and wagged his tail.

He wasn't wearing a collar, but Conrad wasn't even sure they used collars on dogs in New Orleans in 1926.

"I don't have anything to eat," he said. "And I don't have anywhere to live."

The dog stood up, as though he understood, and disappeared up a side street.

Conrad walked a block, but when he turned he saw the dog following him, with a stick in his mouth.

"What?" said Conrad, laughing at the animal.

The dog trotted up to Conrad, dropped the stick at his feet, and then started to run off in expectation.

Conrad kicked the stick into the gutter and carried on walking.

The dog bounced back after it, jumped on the stick, picked it up and followed Conrad some more.

When he stopped again, the dog dropped the stick at his feet again. Conrad stopped down, picked it up, and tossed it a few feet before them.

The dog bounded after it and brought it back, and Conrad couldn't help but smile.

"Come on then, if you want company," he said, and continued on his way, asking his questions as he went, tossing the stick for the dog to fetch at regular intervals.

The dog followed him for about a mile and then, as if a silent whistle had called him, he collected his stick, woofed out of the side of his mouth, and loped off.

Conrad felt almost bereft when the dog had gone, but at least he'd helped to pass the time.

Chapter 25

IT WAS DARK BY THE time Toni and Bart got back to the big house a. A soft drizzle soaked into the dirt and hydrated all of the lush greenery some more. An owl screeched in the distance, mid-hunt. Bats swooped just above their heads. A chorus of toads croaked. And crickets chirruped.

Lights burned behind blinds and curtains at windows. Some flickered behind closed shutters. It was a quiet neighbourhood with little street-life.

The Harley would have alerted everyone within a so-many-yard radius, so they left it between a couple of dumpsters behind one of the commercial buildings, covered with some sacking they found lying around.

They whispered quietly between themselves not wishing to draw attention while local residents minded their own business and got on with their lives in the privacy of their own homes.

"Which house was it again," asked Bart.

"It's the biggest one in the street, at the end of the road," replied Toni. "You can't miss it."

Sure enough, the mansion that looked like it might once have belonged to a governor loomed out of the mizzle, smudged lights behind windows making it glow like a Thomas Kinkade painting. There was no wall around the perimeter, there were no dogs guarding the house, all seemed quiet.

They circled the house until they reached the double gates leading down to the cellar at the back. A wooden bar had been fastened across it, but there were no bolts, no locks, no keys. Just the wooden bar.

"Do you think one of us needs to keep watch?" asked Toni.

"We're not going to be here that long," replied Bart. "We should be able to shift this bar, make sure the doors are free and then get out of here."

All the same, Toni was nervous, so he agreed that she should stay in the yard and keep an eye out for anyone wandering around.

Bart positioned himself and tugged at the bar. It refused to give at first, so he gave it another pull and ended up rolling onto his back with the inertia. But at least he'd removed it.

"Shall we make sure she's still in there?" asked Toni. "It'll be a waste of time if she isn't even here."

"She will have heard me pull the bar out," said Bart. "If she's in there, she'll be on her way out soon enough."

"Okay. But do you want to make sure that the doors will open? We can run away if we hear her."

Bart carefully approached the cellar door again, but he needn't have worried. Before he got there the doors gave once, bounced closed, and were pushed open again. He scurried backwards, on his bum, and hid behind a nearby shrub. The rain seeped through the back of his trousers and the bottom of his shirt, where it hung out below his jacket.

Toni stayed where she was, hidden in the shade of a tree. Bart made sure she was out of sight, then they both watched the cellar doors.

A dishevelled-looking Halima Dominique emerged from the bowels of the house, glancing around as she climbed out of the cellar, either for her captors or for her liberators. Seeing neither, she closed the cellar doors behind her and made her way across the garden.

Toni joined Bart in his hiding place.

"Do you think she'll head for her house?" she whispered.

"Only one way to find out," he replied, starting to follow her.

"But you're wet," hissed Toni. "And dirty. And you've grazed yourself. You're bleeding."

Bart shrugged and carried on after Halima. "That doesn't matter. I can get cleaned up once we get back to the house."

"I suppose if she does go there we could always tell her it was us who let her out," said Toni.

"We might also end up having to tell her a lot more, if that's the case," warned Bart over his shoulder. "But come on," he called. "We'll lose her otherwise."

As they followed her again, it soon became apparent that she wasn't going home at all.

"I think she's heading towards the boat," said Toni.

"I do too," he agreed.

"Perhaps she doesn't feel safe at home."

"Or the boat's neutral territory," suggested Bart.

"Or maybe there's something there that she wants," said Toni suddenly.

The pair kept their usual safe distance behind, with one watching the front and the other watching their rear. They were getting more cautious the longer they stayed in this city.

Bart splashed in a puddle and added a sodden shoe and sock to his ever-increasing list of woes, and Toni tripped over a cobble and almost landed in another puddle, but Bart thrust an arm out to save her.

At the riverside, Halima stopped running. But instead of going towards the boat, looking resplendent with all of its lights on, she turned and went instead to one of the shacks, knocking frantically on the locked door, which in itself was unusual in this usually open town.

A man opened the door, saw Halima, and pulled her inside, closing the door tight behind them.

Bart and Toni followed as far as the door, then pressed themselves against the wooden wall, trying to see in and listen at the window, which was also locked tight against the night.

The voices inside were muffled but they got the gist of the conversation.

Halima told him all about her ordeal and screamed at him asking why he hadn't come to rescue her. He replied that he didn't even know she'd been kidnapped but had wondered where she'd got to. Then, when he asked her how she had got out and she told them someone had unbarred the gates to the cellar, he launched himself at his own door again and stuck his head out, looking to see if she'd been followed. Fortunately, Bart had pre-empted this just in time, grabbed his sister, and pulled her into the shadows at the side of the shack.

Satisfied that there was no one there, the man once again retreated inside and locked the door again behind them.

From the rest of the conversation, which was growing less heated, they learned that Halima would be staying there for tonight at least. It was safe for them to go back to the house and carry on working.

They went back to the big house, collected the motorbike, and drove to Halima Dominique's smaller, friendlier home on the other side of town, and let themselves in.

The components of the time machine sat on the kitchen table hidden beneath a tablecloth they'd found in one of the cupboards. It kept the dust off as well as hiding the equipment from any passing prying eyes.

Bart had his toolkit out and tinkered for a while before admitting that, without the rest of the parts, there was nothing more he could do. He was tinkering for tinkering sake.

Toni took the small bed in the back bedroom while Bart made do with the banquette in the front room. And there they passed a relatively peaceful, undisturbed night.

HONDO PITTS SAT AT his work desk in one of the downstairs rooms threading different coloured glass beads onto a length of catgut. In the background a radio quietly broadcast a musical show.

Upstairs a frustrated Conrad paced up and down, from room to room. He could just make out the radio too, but he wasn't listening. Inside his head he plotted against the brother and sister who were helping his own brother hold onto the company that should rightfully be his. He'd worked out the perfect plan, had gone back in time to change the time continuum thingy, but his brother had caught on, or been warned, or just plain noticed that something wasn't quite right. And so he had sent the gruesome twosome back in time to fix it. Conrad had thought they'd be elsewhere by now and unable to do anything to help. So when they'd turned up in his shadow, they'd taken him totally by surprise and he'd had to act on the hop.

Now everything was going wrong. His own time machine wouldn't work without those cogs. The amulet he'd come back for in the first place and given to Hondo Pitts for safekeeping had been stolen. The woman who had the other amulet had disappeared off the face of the earth. And someone had knocked him out when he'd followed the actress home. He wondered who that could be as it clearly hadn't been Bart. Or Pitts. Either someone else wanted the actress for something, or they were protecting her.

Tomorrow was the day that he needed to stop her getting arrested at the mardi gras. But he didn't know where she was. If he didn't do it this time, though, he supposed he could always come back... supposing, of course, that he could get back to the future to come back from.

It was all very complicated and difficult when it should have been so easy, so quick, so simple. His brother was far too clever for his own good. But at least he had the element of surprise over his colleagues. They'd had no idea where they were, when it was or why they were here. They wouldn't have had chance to do any research before getting here, so all he had to bank on now was their ignorance.

Hopefully, they had no idea what had happened or what they needed to do to fix it. Hopefully, he had the advantage. Hopefully all would work out in the end. Hopefully everything would fall in to place tomorrow.

Chapter 26

BART PACKED EVERYTHING he needed into his satchel. The weather didn't look very thundery, but even if it did, they were still short a few essential items. So, while it was still dark, he took his satchel, his motorbike and a small pocket torch to where the boat was docked on the river. Toni stayed at the house, partly to hold the fort but also to see if Halima Dominique returned. And anyway, she wanted a lie-in before the day's adventures – it was going to be a long day as it was and she'd need all of her energy.

She lay on the bed in the back of the house and listened in the darkness to the motorbike as her brother drove off into the night. Actually, it was morning, but it was still very dark and it was still very early. He'd taken the chiming clock to pieces so she only had her watch to rely on. He'd put the bits he needed in with his other guff and left the rest of the clock spread out on the kitchen table.

Toni tossed and turned for a while and probably even dozed, but she couldn't really settle. So she got up to make a breakfast of scrambled eggs and toast. She made herself some black coffee too. She preferred tea but couldn't stand it without milk, whereas she didn't mind coffee without milk. The milk they'd bought yesterday smelt a bit ripe and she didn't want to risk it.

With nothing to do and a cannibalised radio she couldn't listen to, Toni went back to the bed, pulled a notebook and pencil from one of her pockets, and started to write a journal.

THE STREETS WERE FAIRLY empty at this time of the morning. The occasional worker was up, sweeping the streets, emptying the bins, extinguishing the streetlights. Some were making their way to their place of work. Most were still indoors, curtains, blinds and shutters closed against the dark and the apparently incoming storm. Soon everybody would be up to make final preparations for the Mardi Gras. Until then, he had the place to himself. The first parades would begin mid-morning to early-afternoon.

The streets were pretty much ready, aside from a few repairs following the recent storms. And the dockside was all of a bustle, compared to the rest of the city he'd passed through. Shutters on houses and all exterior paintwork was looking its best. Flowers still in bloom decorated the railings, balconies, pillars, walls and windows. Windows not covered with shutters glistened. Washing lines had been brought in. Everywhere looked spic and span.

Bart parked the bike behind some crates and covered it with a large piece of sacking. He'd already immobilised it. He hitched the satchel strap onto his shoulder and wandered as though aimlessly. He didn't want to make a beeline for the boat in case he was spotted. Instead he moseyed around, looking interested in the various shops, stores and businesses that weren't open yet.

The gangplank was in place and there didn't seem to be anyone guarding it, so he nonchalantly made his way up it, along a white-painted outer deck, down some steps, and along a few corridors until he found the concert room – or whatever they called it on a boat. Show lounge? Theatre? The safety curtain was down but he could still get to the footlights. He disconnected one and took it behind the privacy of the safety curtain, where he thought he'd be alone.

Two men were painting scenery and a third was repairing the banister on a wooden staircase. He had a pot of paint at his feet. They nodded good morning to him and got on with their work. Perhaps they thought he was the electrician. He dismantled the footlight, took out the bulb, the mirror, and a few other connections, then he put it all back together as best as he could. He nodded farewell to the other workers, slipped in front of the safety curtain again, replaced the light, and tripped out of the concert room again.

With hardly anybody about he was able to explore the rest of the boat at his leisure, finding his way down the stairs to another deck. This must have been where the players lived when they were on the road – or on the river. Some of the doors had numbers. Some of them rather helpfully had names on them. Sadly, he couldn't find a name for Miss Halima Dominique.

He found an office in which was a huge ledger sat in an unlocked cupboard. This had lists of names, lots of other details, and in the final column a monetary figure. He wasn't sure if this was a record of the performers, the crew, the passengers, or just a bought or sold ledger. So he adjusted an oil lamp on the desk, settled down and started to read.

The fancy scrawl was difficult to read in the dim light, especially when the ink started to run out of the pen they were using. But he persevered and worked out that there were different sections of the ledger for different activities. And there she was:

Dominique, Halima – vaudeville – singer – 39

Did that mean her cabin was number 39? There was only one way to find out.

He went back to the residential part of the boat and found a cabin with the number 39 on. The door was unlocked, and inside were three cabin beds, all set at different angles. Three women shared this cabin, one of them may have been Halima Dominique. He went back to the office to see what else he could find, but all he came up with were some flyers for the following few days' programmes.

The vaudeville section was due at four o'clock for the matinee performance, and nine o'clock for the evening performance. There didn't seem to be any other performances scheduled, but the programme was the same for the whole of Mardi Gras. That meant that

Halima had to be back at work in the afternoon. She would probably be back here by four o'clock at the latest, if they didn't have any rehearsals.

He left the boat and walked up and down her side on the dock, surprised to see another much smaller boat almost nudging up against it. A young lad was swilling the deck of the smaller boat and saw Bart watching. He called out a greeting and Bart replied.

"What boat is this?" he asked.

"This is the boat that pushes the showboat along the river," said the lad.

"Oh?" said Bart, surprised. "I thought it was a paddle steamer."

"No, boss. The theatre takes up too much room where the engine would normally go. So these showboats need another boat to move them around."

"Does anyone live on this boat?"

"Only the crew."

"No passengers?"

The lad shook his head. "Jus' crew, boss."

Bart thanked him and tossed a dime at him, which the lad expertly caught.

"Thank 'um boss," he said, with a smile, pocketing the coin and getting back to his early morning chores.

Bart strolled along the shacks and shanties that lined the dockside, giving the one Halima had gone into the night before a wide berth.

Aside from the chemicals, he had everything he needed other than the radio antenna. The chemicals he could get from the photographer's flash gun. He cast his eyes around the dock to see if there was a likely place to find a rod. His lightning conductor.

He could only think of an engine room, and the showboat didn't have one of those, apparently. He looked up at the funnels that weren't actually connected to anything. A flag hung at full mast with another one further down the pole... and then the light-bulb went on over his head again.

The flagpole.

He clambered aboard the boat again and climbed up onto the top of the bridge where he could just about reach the rope that the two flags flew from. Using this, he pulled himself up and towards the flagpole base, which was secured with four nuts. They were very tight. Too tight for him to undo without taking a long time about it and drawing attention to himself.

He dropped back onto the bridge, falling against the railing that ran around the edge of the bridge roof. And he felt it move behind him.

He turned his attention from the flagpole to the railings behind him, which were very badly maintained and at least needed a fresh coat of paint. The railing along the top was crooked. He pushed it, and it moved again. It wasn't fastened.

The length of pole was only about five feet long, but that was probably all he needed. And it unscrewed very easily if he pushed the uprights slightly apart.

The railing gave with a clatter and he caught it before it fell overboard and into the murky depths of the Mississippi.

Armed with his latest pickings, he turned to jump back down the ladder.

However, there was a man waiting on the deck below with a gun in his hand pointing directly at Bart.

Chapter 27

TONI CHECKED HER WATCH. It would soon be time for her to go and meet her brother at Veronique's house. They hadn't told her they wouldn't be back the previous night and Toni was feeling guilty. Besides, they still had a key. Not that they needed it. Just like almost everyone else in the town, Veronique didn't bother locking her door.

"If anyone wants anything, they'll get in anyway," she'd said. "There's no reason for them to destroy everything in the way in the meantime."

Toni skipped along, carrying her belongings in the carpet bag. She'd helped herself to anything that looked useful. But everything else was hers or Bart's – or Conrad's, she remembered guiltily, thinking of the cogs that were apparently of no use whatsoever to her or Bart.

When she reached Veronique's brightly coloured door, she was greeted by the cheerful face of the fruit-seller. Toni had made her a little corn dolly-type trinket out of some of the things she'd found in Halima's house and she hoped that Veronique would appreciate the little thank you gift. She'd made a similar one for Odette too, and a smaller one for Esme. Gideon and Desmond were harder to gauge, but she hoped she might find something for them at the Mardi Gras itself. "Come in, come in!" said Veronique, opening the door and gesturing for Toni to follow her into the house. "You found somewhere to stay last night?" she asked.

"Yes, I'm sorry we didn't let you know–"

"Hush, chile, it's fine."

Toni gave her the key, and thanked her. When Toni held out the corn dolly, the older woman seemed delighted and promised to treasure it forever.

"You and your brother, you're leaving today, yes?" she asked.

"Hopefully, if all goes well, yes."

"You have repaired your vehicle?" Toni nodded. "That is good. You will stay for some of the fiesta, though?"

"Oh yes," said Toni. "We don't want to miss that."

"Good, because I know that my sister and her family would like to say goodbye to you too."

"And we want to say goodbye and thank you to them too."

Veronique led Toni to the back of the house. Her back room was like her best parlour. And she sat Toni down while she went to make coffee.

"Where is your brother?" asked Veronique from the kitchen.

"I thought he might be here," replied Toni. "He's supposed to be meeting me here. I take it he hasn't been yet?" she asked.

"No, I have not seen him. What time did he say he'd be here?"

Toni looked at the clock on the wall. "He was supposed to be here ten minutes ago. I'm already late."

"I expect he will be here very soon," said Veronique, placing the coffee in front of Toni along with a plate of small titbits.

Toni hoped so, but a shiver ran down her spine all the same.

CONRAD BUSTLED HONDO Pitts out of the apartment and into the town. The boy was waiting for them in the alley way, and together the three of them made their way into town, Pitts breaking off briefly to feed the alligators.

Once the beasts were fed, Hondo went and gathered three rolls of beads. One roll, the biggest, he placed around his own neck. The smallest of the piles he gave to the boy. The medium-sized roll he gave to Conrad, who looked at is as though it was something he'd walked in on the street.

"What do you want me to do with that?" he asked, incredulous.

"Do you want to fit in or do you want to stand out?"

Conrad tutted and sighed but took the beads anyway and hung them around his neck. He could feel the weight of them all and was surprised. They were a lot heavier than they looked when there were so many of them together.

They did keep getting stopped on the way as people bought beads from them. Some tried to haggle, but Pitts was having none of that. Even the boy sold some, but Conrad's seemed to be for restocking for when the other two needed more.

"It's the best day for these," said Hondo Pitts. "Well, today onwards. Sometimes at the end of Mardi Gras they think they can buy them cheap. But I just put them into the storeroom until next time. It's not as if they'll go off, is it?"

They slowly made their way to the dock.

There the showboat sat on the water, looking just as resplendent as the rest of the town with all of her finery. Crew and company were milling around, doing their bit, smiles and cheerful faces painted on, literally. The smell of greasepaint and perfume and talc mingled with the usual smells of the murky river.

And there she was, Miss Halima Dominique, firmly on the arm of the master of ceremonies, who was also wearing his performing best. Miss Dominique looked beautiful in a scarlet, drop-waisted satin dress and a long-line fur coat draped over her shoulders to keep her warm. A hair band around her head held a feather in place and around her neck hung the amulet.

Conrad's mouth almost watered at the sight – not of the beautiful woman, but of the striking pendant against her breast.

He grabbed hold of Hondo Pitts, who was just in the middle of another sale and didn't take too kindly to being either manhandled or interrupted. But he relaxed when he saw what the other man was staring at.

"Calm down, boss," he hissed, nodding towards the sheriff's men who were on the prowl.

Conrad tried to contain his excitement, but everything else had so far gone so wrong, he really needed this to go right today.

He had to stop her getting arrested.

And then he had to get that amulet from around her neck.

Of Toni and Bart, there was no sign.

BART WAS ON THE FLOOR of the shack Miss Dominique had taken refuge in the night before. His hands and feet were tied with rope, and he'd been searched, but he'd not been hurt – or not beyond his pride. The man with the gun was the man who had opened the door to her. He spoke with a rough, French accent.

"What you want with Miss Halima?" asked the man.

"I wanted the flagpole," said Bart, "but I had to make do with the handrail from around the roof."

"I watch you," said the man. "You went to Miss Halima's room and searched her things. What you want with Miss Halima?"

"I wondered if she had a necklace. We have the pair and my sister saw her with it and we wondered if she'd left it in her cabin," Bart half-lied, thinking on his feet – or, rather, on his backside. "But we think she may be in trouble."

"You no her slave master?"

"No. I'm not her slave master."

"Miss Halima, she need help," said the man.

"She does?" asked Bart, wriggling into a more comfortable seated position.

"She has the problem with the..." he cast around for the right word but decided on sign language instead, mimicking drinking with his hand.

"Booze?" suggested Bart.

"Yes, the booze as you say. And the smoke?" Again, he did sign language for smoking a pipe – a big pipe.

"Yes, smoking," agreed Bart.

"She need help. Or she kill herself. And she need help or her slave master take her back."

"I thought slavery was abolished sixty years ago," said Bart.

"Not here in Louisiana," said the man. "The ol' families. They still keep their slaves, but they call them servants. They mek them buy the'selves out, but most can't afford it. Miss Halima, she bin gone a year and a day. They shunt a took her back, but they did. She need help," he said again.

"We can help her..." ventured Bart.

"How you do that?"

"We can get her taken away and put in a safe place."

"Will that mek Miss Halima well again?"

Bart nodded. "And it will keep her safe from her slave master. And you might still be able to visit her."

"I no care about that, so long as she well and safe. How you do this?"

"Do the booze or drugs make her violent?"

The man thought for a moment. "Yes'm. Sometimes."

"Well, if we can upset her so that she attacks someone, while the sheriff's men are here, they might arrest her."

The man stepped back. "I no want her arrested!"

"No, it will be temporary. But they will put her in a hospital, where they can care for her, get her off the booze and laudanum, keep her safe from the slave boss too."

Bart felt sorry for the poor man. He seemed torn. Keep her free and she'd never be free – of either the substances or her old master. Lock her up and she'd be free from those, but not free herself. He was between a rock and a hard place.

"We could give her the gun," he suggested. "If she wave the gun they may take her too."

"But she may also hurt someone—"

The man's face broke into a gap-toothed grin. "She no hurt anyone. It no real." To prove it, he picked the gun up from the table and showed it to Bart.

It was a replica.

"The name's Bart, by the way."

"Bart? That is strange name."

"It's short for Bartholomew."

The man tried to say it but gave up. "I call you Bart," he laughed. "Koofrey Carbonneau," said the man. "But you can call me Koof," he added as Bart tried to roll the name around his mouth and failed.

He untied Bart's hands and feet.

Chapter 28

CONRAD, HONDO PITTS and the boy roamed around the dockside keeping a very firm eye on Miss Halima Dominique and her escort. But they weren't the only ones watching her.

The two men who had taken her to the big house had noticed that she was missing, and they thought they knew exactly where to find her. They'd searched and searched from very early this morning, but she wasn't on the boat and she wasn't with the rest of the ensemble. Then, all of a sudden, when there were too many eyes around, she'd appeared, in all of her finery. But not from the boat. She'd come from a different part of the town, a different part of the dock, and they'd not seen from where, which would have been useful if she disappeared again. When they caught her this time, it had to be for good.

They watched her and the MC from the show as they paraded around, chatted to folk. And every so often they saw her sneak a drink from a small bottle she carried in her equally small bag. Trying not to look too conspicuous themselves, they clearly failed when Halima Dominique spotted them and whispered something into her companion's ear, who also looked towards them. Because she was too busy watching them, she didn't see the other group of people who were clearly interested in her. But the two men watching her had seen them.

The bead-sellers and the boy stayed as close to her as they possibly could. Watching, following, whispering. Then they noticed someone else was watching her. Well, one of them was watching her, the other one was staring right at them.

This wasn't going to end good.

The two men decided to slope off, but Koofrey Carbonneau wasn't about to let them do that. He touched Bart on the shoulder, who turned to see where he was pointing. And then they started to follow the two strangers. Who decided to hedge their bets and stand their ground after all.

"You leave Miss Halima alone," said Koof.

"She's our property," said the bigger of the two men.

"She was away a year and a day. She no longer anyone's property."

"And anyway," said Bart. "Slavery's illegal now and has been for years."

"She's not a slave. She's our servant."

"So you pay her a wage and she's free to go as and when she likes?" asked Bart.

"That's not how it works here. She's our property."

"And how it works here is if she manages to stay away for a year and a day, then she's free."

The two men looked at each other, then the big one continued.

"It hasn't been a year."

"Was a year and a day the day the boat was due in," said Koof. "But the boat was a day late. It's been gone all that time and Miss Halima was on it when it left."

The bigger of the two looked puzzled, but the other one wasn't having any of it.

"She's ours and she's coming with us," he said, rushing towards Halima and the MC.

The MC placed a protective arm around Miss Halima's shoulders, but Miss Halima looked over to the sheriff's men and called out to them.

Within moments there was a scuffle going on with Miss Halima being pulled from the MC to Koof to a deputy to one or the other of the two men.

Bart didn't know if this was how he was supposed to let Halima be arrested. But he doubted it meant her being taken back to the big house again. He also doubted it meant being carted off to the local jail, but so far she wasn't causing a scene, or not enough to be arrested, and especially when she was the victim.

But the sheriff's men were white and the big men were white and Halima and the MC and Koof were all black. Bart remembered hearing many cases of racism between the police and the black community and even the Ku Klux Klan. So he doubted that Miss Halima would be treated very fairly. But he'd promised Koof he'd help her.

By now Conrad and the bead-seller had joined them, with Conrad trying to placate everyone. He and Bart acknowledged each other, but they were both plainly interested in the same thing. Conrad did seem to be pouring oil on, though. Perhaps he and Toni had read him wrong after all.

Bart could see that Miss Halima was getting agitated, so he pulled her free and as he did so retrieved the fake gun from his pocket and gave it to her.

The alcohol she'd consumed so far today already made her very unstable. As soon as she noticed she had a gun, she started to wave it at everyone while screaming like a banshee for them all to leave her alone. Not just those around her hit the deck. Everyone within the vicinity did, and like a wave of water it spread around the dockside.

"Leave me alone!" she yelled. "I shoot!"

When Conrad noticed that Bart and his mate hadn't dropped to the ground, he started to stand up too.

"Come on now, miss," he said. "You don't want to hurt anyone."

"They want to put me in prison again!" she cried. "I no theirs. I free. I on showboat for a year and a day. I free!"

"I'm sure they'll understand that, miss, if you tell them calmly and quietly. You don't need the gun."

He continued to walk towards her and eventually those watching lifted their heads from the floor too, and slowly stood up again.

Halima stopped waving the gun around and pointed it at Conrad instead.

"Go away! I shoot!" she said.

But he paid no attention.

As she tried to pull the trigger, and failed, realisation swamped over her and she started to scream and wail again.

"Shush, shush, miss," urged Conrad.

She started to cry and she threw the gun at Conrad. Then she started to pull and rip at her beautifully coiffured hair.

Her MC tried to calm her down. The two men who had come to steal her tried to calm her down. The police tried to calm her down. Even Hondo Pitts the bead-seller tried to calm her down. They all failed miserably and had to watch out for sharp fingernails scratching, teeth biting, and small fists thumping.

Bart and Koof just watched. Koof wanted to go to her but he stayed at Bart's side.

The sheriff's men approached with caution. Between them and Bart they were able to catch her and hold her still until she calmed down. When she'd stopped keening, they escorted her away, asking the MC to accompany them.

"But I have a show to put on," complained the MC.

"I go," said Koof.

The deputies looked at Halima and she nodded, resigned. They let go of one of her arms so she could hold her hand out to her friend.

Bart stooped in the dirt and picked up the fake gun, causing the crowd to jump again, until they remembered that it was a fake.

"Here," he said to Koof.

"You have it, my friend," said Koof. He trailed sadly after the little huddle heading to the nearest jail.

"Surely you don't need to arrest her?" said Conrad, but they ignored him. "Wait!" he cried, and they turned. "She has my property. She stole it." They all looked at him, puzzled. "The charm around her neck. It's mine."

Halima let go of Koof's hand and pressed it to the amulet, shaking her head. But one of the deputies ripped it from around her neck and threw it into the dirt.

As Conrad stooped to pick it up, Bart was sure he had a smirk on his face. But he was quick to wipe it off when he presented himself to the crowd again. "Such a shame," he muttered. He turned to Bart and pointed at him. "And you have something of mine too."

One of the deputies paused and turned to see what Conrad was on about this time. But his colleague called him and they finally disappeared into the town.

Bart sighed. "I don't have anything of yours," he said.

TONI AND VERONIQUE made the decision to go on to the street festival anyway. On the way they collected Desmond and Odette and the children. Odette and Esme were very happy with their corn dollies, and Toni promised Desmond and Gideon that they would get something too.

Desmond looked absolutely wonderful in his witch-doctor outfit, with coloured feathers floating in the breeze and red and black face paint rendering him almost impossible to recognise. Odette had her hair braided and she wore a pert little hat and a bright purple feather boa over her gold sparkly outfit. Esme and Gideon were dressed in bright colours with what looked like dyed handkerchiefs pulled back over their heads that they could turn into masks when the parade started. Veronique was a vision in scarlet with a turban on her head and a double string of fat beads around her neck.

"I feel quite under-dressed," complained Toni, laughing.

"In that outfit?" squealed Desmond.

She was wearing her black taffeta skirt and her royal blue satin shirt, her black corset-like bodice over the top of her outfit, pinching her in at the waist, and her very fine top hat. And her long hair curled down to her waist.

"I think you look splendid!" said Odette. "Perfect."

The streets were starting to fill up as everyone made their way to the parade.

"I don't want to go without Bart," she said, looking one way then the other for her brother.

"Then you won't have to," beamed Veronique. He was coming towards them, looking slightly the worse for wear in his work clothes and with his satchel over his shoulder.

Chapter 29

"RIGHT THEN!" SHOUTED the MC, clapping his gloved hands together. "Let's get this show on the road. Roll up, roll up. Free shows on the showboat today after the main parade. Get your tickets early. Or there won't be room."

He wandered off, completely ignoring Bart, Conrad, Hondo and the others who had joined them all. A small cluster of people followed him, hoping to get some good tickets for the unusually free show later this afternoon.

Bart had already started to leave, but Conrad didn't want to lose him again. He was pleased to see that he was heading towards Toni.

"Ah, Antoinette," he murmured.

"Boss?" said Hondo Pitts.

"Don't call me that," hissed Conrad. "I've told you before."

"Sorry, boss."

"Do you know who that dog belongs to?" he asked, spotting the white dog. Hondo shook his head, so Conrad shrugged his shoulders and ignored the creature.

As he approached Bart and Toni and, obviously, their friends, the brother and sister greeted each other as though they hadn't seen each other for years.

"Do you know who those people are?" he asked Hondo Pitts.

"The lady in red is Missus Veronique. She's a fruit-seller. The woman in the feather boa is her sister Odette, which means the man in the bright feathers is probably Odette's husband, Desmond the witch-doctor. The children are theirs. I don't know their names."

"Do they all live together?"

"I don't think so, boss."

Conrad approached the crowd and opened his arms in recognition and welcome. "Antoinette! Bartholomew! Here we all are."

Toni glanced over at him and burst out laughing.

"Nice necklace, Conrad."

Damn! He'd forgotten the beads. He took what was left of Hondo's wares from around his neck and gave them to the boy. He saw Toni give the boy a double take. Hmm, she knew him too. He turned to Hondo Pitts to give him a quizzical look.

"She must have seen him following her," said Pitts, holding his hands out in surrender. "No harm done."

"I think you have something of mine," he said to Toni. She looked at the necklace in his hand.

"What do you mean?" asked Bart.

"Your little sister stole something of mine from the Model T Ford." He turned back to Toni. "Didn't you, sweet pea?"

Toni had a rummage in her bag and came up with the cogs. "I thought they might help us fix the time machine on the Harley," she said, holding them out to him. "But we didn't need them in the end."

"Oh?" said Conrad, taking them from her. "Have you repaired it, then?"

"Not yet," said Bart. But we have almost everything that we need." He started to look around the crowd to see if he recognised someone. Conrad didn't know who he was looking for.

Conrad raised an eyebrow. "Interesting." His eyes alighted on the rod Bart held in his free hand. "You have scaffolding?" he said.

Bart looked down and agreed that yes, it would make a very good scaffolding pole. To his sister he said, "Have you seen the photographer, Toni? Don't forget you wanted him to take a picture of us all."

"Oh yes," said Toni. "I'd forgotten, but no I haven't seen him." She turned to their friends. "We'd love to have our picture taken with you all," she said. "Then our picture can be our thank you gift to you,

Desmond, for all of your help." She indicated the scratch on her forehead that no longer needed a dressing. "That ointment of yours works like magic," she said. Then, to Conrad, "Do you have everything you want now?"

"Apart from you, sweet pea," he said, lasciviously.

"Ugh," she shuddered, and went after her brother, their friends towing along and giving Conrad a polite nod but a wide berth.

"WHEN WE HAVE OUR PICTURE taken," she said, chattering, to the others, we'll have to give him your details and then we can tell you where to leave our copy so we can pick it up later." She was referring, of course, to some kind of time capsule that she and Bart could find when they returned to their own time. Or, they could always come back for it.

The group was quite excited and had no trouble leaving Conrad and his friends behind.

"One moment, miss," said a voice.

Toni turned to see Hondo Pitts coming towards her.

"Would you like some beads? For the Mardi Gras?"

Toni looked around and saw lots of people were wearing single strings of beads, sometimes double like Veronique, but most were like the ones Hondo Pitts was selling.

"Yes please," she said. She bought a string of beads for her and a string of beads for Gideon, who proudly hung them around his neck and beamed a dazzlingly white smile at her.

THEY ALL TRAILED AFTER Bart, who was loping along at quite the gait. He kept on looking at the sky. It would have been good if the boss had given them a time to aim at because, at the moment, there didn't seem to be any sign of a storm.

He'd spotted the photographer, who had set up a mini photo-booth-type area in a corner of the dock. His camera was directed towards the river where the huge showboat was in the background. There was a queue of people waiting to use his services. Bart hoped that the man would be happy to do business.

"He's over here," he called behind him to Toni and the others, who weren't keeping up particularly well. When he reached the queue, he took his place and waited for them to join him.

Once Toni and the others were able to hold their place in the queue for him, he peeled off and chatted to the photographer as he worked, asking pertinent questions, complimenting him on his chosen backdrop and so on. Then, when it was their turn, he paid for the group shot and asked for three copies to be sent to Desmond's address.

The seven of them clustered in a group with the mighty showboat behind them and they all fixed beaming smiles on their faces while they waited for the flashgun to go off. Then Bart chatted some more with the photographer, paid him extra, and came away with small amounts of the chemicals he needed. The photographer didn't even ask him what he wanted it for.

"I think that's us done here," Bart said to Toni, after thanking the photographer. He turned to their friends. "The photographer will bring all three copies to Desmond's house," said Bart, "and then you can let Veronique have her copy."

"What should we do with your copy?" asked Odette. "Take it to the post office? Do you have an address we can use?"

Bart scratched his head and looked at his sister. They hadn't thought this through properly yet, had they?

Toni had one of her light-bulb moments. "Do you have a monument in any of the cemeteries?"

"No," said Odette.

"But we do have a plaque on the wall in the old cemetery," said her sister.

"Great," said Bart. "Does it have a chamber behind it?"

"I think so," said Veronique.

"Could you leave it there for us?" asked Toni. "We don't know when we might be back but in case we don't have chance to drop in to see you all..."

"Yes, yes," said Odette. "We can do that."

"But of course, you must still try to come and visit us when you do come back," said Veronique.

"Cool," said Bart.

CONRAD AND HONDO PITTS left the party, with the boy and the dog trailing behind. They made their way through the packed streets, which were getting fuller now, to the old cemetery where Conrad was keeping his machine parked. On the way, Hondo and the boy made many more sales of beads, and Hondo even let the boy keep some of his money.

Conrad clasped the amulet tightly. Hand and charm were both in the pocket of his coat.

When they got to the cemetery, Hondo and the boy stayed outside and continued to sell beads to the passers-by, leaving Conrad to do what he had to do.

He moved the stone aside and inched into the space between the car and the wall of the tomb. He didn't have a lot of room and hardly any light. But he knew his machine very well and was able to work.

He stripped off his coat, removed his hat, rolled up his sleeves and set to work lifting the floorboards on the passenger side of the car. There, in the box, he stowed the amulet, clicking it into a special place designed to engage it securely during time travel. He packed the box away again, making sure the floorboards were securely fixed down. It wouldn't be long before he was heading home now, and the immobiliser was still in place until then anyway.

He opened the glove compartment to reveal the mechanism for the time machine. He fixed the two cogs in place, set everything into motion, then closed and locked the glove compartment.

With everything primed, all he had to do was insert his ignition key, press the starter motor and push down the clutch pedal with is foot. Then the vortex would start and he'd be on his way.

He stepped out of the vehicle into the tight space again, and this time locked the door securely, making sure the other door and the boot were also locked. Then he stepped outside of the tomb, rolled the stone over, and returned to Hondo Pitts.

They all went back to Hondo's place to replenish his bead supply, get something to eat, feed the alligators, and conclude their business. Conrad was to pay him in several gold coins for his services, and he promised to look him up next time he was in the area.

As Conrad made his way through the streets, the first big spots of rain slowly began to fall. He looked up at the darkening sky and sniffed at the air. There was another humdinger on the way, but this time he'd be long gone before it arrived.

Chapter 30

BART WAS UP TO HIS elbows under the seat of the Harley, which flicked up into a right angle and revealed the time machine mechanism beneath it. It was dark inside the tomb, so Toni dug into her bag for her mini torch.

The rod was propped up against the wall. The bits out of the clock and the radio were laid out on a cloth on a shelf inside the tomb. The chemical powders were being kept dry in two little pouches that the photographer had let them have.

Bart saved the chemicals for when the machine was definitely working, but he was using his toolkit to add each of the parts to the main mechanism.

"It needs a spark for the powders, he said.

"Like a lighter or a match?" asked Toni.

"No, like a flint or something. But we don't have a flint."

"A stone age flint or a flint from a lighter?"

"Yes, anything like that. But not a flame. It needs to be a spark.

He got all of the bits connected and tested it. He closed the seat, climbed onto the bike and jumped onto the kickstart. The engine turned over and fired up, but that was all. He shook his head, switching the engine off again.

They wheeled the motorbike out into the open where they could take advantage of the remaining light and even the rain didn't stop them doing what they needed to do.

Bart had another go at making sure all the components were in the right place. But still it wasn't doing what he wanted it to.

He fastened the lightning rod to the electrics, pulled the mechanism to pieces one more time, and carefully and methodically put all the components back in, cleaning the connections, making sure there were no breaks in the wires, testing that everything worked before he added it.

He tried to fire it up again, but failed.

"We need a flint," he said to Toni.

Toni tried to think where she'd seen a lighter – or where indeed she'd seen any matches.

Bart rummaged in his coat pocket and pulled out the replica gun, holding it in the air in triumph. "This has a firing pin," he announced. He dismantled the gun, pulled out the firing pin, then wondered where he was supposed to put it. He fitted the firing pin in a few places before deciding where it was supposed to go. Then he nodded, stroked his chin, and said, "We'll get one pop at this now. If it doesn't work, we're stuck."

The spots of rain grew heavier and the sky clouded over. There was a very quiet rumble of thunder in the distance. Downtown they could hear the party getting into full swing. They would put up awnings if the rain grew too heavy. Birds stopped singing, however, and the sky turned a cloudy purple.

"We don't have long," said Toni. "We have to get out to the delta yet."

Bart climbed onto the motorbike, gave it a kick, and the engine burst into life again. He checked some dials, climbed off the bike again, lifted the seat, checked a few things and looked at his sister with a frown.

"That's it," he said. "We've done it." He waited a beat for Toni to realise what he was saying, and as the smile crept across her face he said it again. "We did it!"

"Great!" said Toni. "Can we go now?"

"Yup," said Bart. He closed the seat, adjusted something on his dashboard, and placed the rod inside the side-car. "I'll connect that when we get out to the delta," he said.

Toni settled into the side-car, fixed her seatbelt and put on her helmet and goggles. Her brother glared at her until she had also fastened the strap beneath her chin tightly. Nodding, he climbed aboard again, put his own helmet on, and did up his jacket.

He changed gear, opened the throttle, and sped off towards the delta.

The streets on this side of town were almost empty. Everyone was at the fiesta, apart from the odd stray dog taking advantage of unattended rubbish bins with food in.

As they left the town and drove out onto the dirt track, the heavens opened. They only had a few minutes to get to the delta and the rain made visibility difficult. They had to slow down when the reached the crash site, but once they were sure, they came to a standstill.

Bart fixed the lightning rod while Toni lifted the floorboards in the side-car and opened the stash box. She removed all of the trinkets and odds and sods that she kept in there to reveal at the very bottom the engaging mechanism. She took the amulet, Conrad's amulet, and fastened it into place, twisting it until it engaged and the light came on. When she was happy the artefact was secure and registered, she piled everything back into place on top of it, refixed the floorboards, and settled back into her seat.

Ready to go, they assumed their positions and waited for the storm to arrive.

Chapter 31

BACK IN TOWN, IN THE oldest cemetery in New Orleans, Conrad fired up his machine, braced himself, and was off.

The eddy picked up speed as it sucked the vehicle down and into its depths. Down, down, down, until Conrad couldn't breathe properly. Suddenly there was a bump, restarting the supply of oxygen, and Conrad relaxed.

He felt another bump as the colours changed from white silver to white gold, to yellow, to orange. The specks of dust turned into little stars, then big stars, then planets. As the vortex continued to swirl, Conrad became aware of a high-pitched whining noise he'd never heard before. He went into a mild panic thinking that something must have gone wrong – those pesky interfering interlopers must have sabotaged his time machine in revenge.

But the whining stopped for a moment and changed to a whimpering, and Conrad felt hot breath on the back of his neck.

He turned in his seat slowly not knowing what to expect, and almost jumped out of his skin to see a pair of eyes peering frantically into his.

Then he laughed as he realised it was a dog – the stray dog that had been following him, the same dog he'd thrown a stick for only the day before. His laughter of relief changed to disbelief and then slight outrage before he was horrified.

He'd never had a pet before, didn't even like dogs that much. What was he supposed to do with this one?

Conrad didn't have much time to decide what to do. He knew he could keep it or he could go back another day and take it back. Or he could just kick it out when he got home and let it fend for itself.

Whichever, he didn't have time to do anything now. He couldn't abort the journey. He'd make his decision in a day or so... after he'd lived with it for a while.

Conrad smiled at the dog and stroked its head.

"Don't worry, little tramp," he said. "It'll all be over in a moment."

He turned to concentrate on the matter in hand again.

As the lights started to disappear, Conrad felt the first bounce, then the second, and then one more before finally landing back at home base. All went quiet and still and black. They'd arrived at their destination. Conrad was home.

BART AND TONI WATCHED as the swirling storm approached. Across the delta they could see a funnel that had picked up all sorts of debris. Trees and houses were swirling around before disappearing into the centre of the maelstrom. The funnel was going in a different direction to where they were, but they were still able to watch it as it crossed the open land, whipping up water and more rubbish as it went.

The electric storm followed it. Again, they watched the lightning fork between murky sky and dusty land, and they heard the thunder rumble a few seconds later. As the thunder followed the lightning ever closer, Bart counted the seconds. He checked the dial on his motorbike dashboard. It was just after four o'clock.

He monitored the storm, to make sure it was coming towards them, and he calculated its speed and actual direction.

He turned to his sister and shouted to her. "Are you ready?"

She held onto the sides of the side-car with her fingers until her knuckles turned white with the effort. She nodded and held her breath.

Bart pulled his goggles down one last time, revved the engine a few times, checked over his shoulder to ensure the funnel was behind him, then he opened the throttle and sped into the oncoming electric storm.

The milometer crept up – thirty miles an hour, forty miles an hour, sixty miles an hour, seventy-five – then one almighty flash of lightning struck their lightning rod and, after a bit of a trip and a rumble, all of the lights started to flash.

The eddy picked up speed as it sucked them both down and into its depths. Down, down, down, until they couldn't breathe properly, until they thought they'd never breathe again.

He felt another bump as the colours changed from white silver to white gold, to yellow, to orange. The specks of dust turned into little stars, then big stars, then planets, as they reached their programmed destination.

Bart squeezed Toni's hand as the darkness closed in around them. He felt the first bounce, then the second, and then one more before they finally landed. And then all went quiet and still and black.

They'd arrived.

BACK HOME IN HIS NORMAL garden at the back of his normal house in his normal neighbourhood and in his normal time zone, Conrad picked up a stick that lay on the ground at the foot of a tree. He looked at it, taking in all of its texture and feeling.

Then he pulled his arm back and threw the stick as far as he could. Away it flew, along the length of his low-maintenance but long patch of land, sailing through the air against a winter blue sky. As it bumped and bounced before coming in to land, the dog went flying after it as fast as he could, tongue hanging out in pure pleasure, panting his head off, as if laughing out loud.

When he fetched the stick back and dropped it at Conrad's feet, jumping backwards and forwards, waiting for Conrad to pick it up and throw it again, Conrad felt a stupidly mad rush of happiness and pride.

He picked up the stick again and sent it off into its orbit again, closely followed by the speeding dog.

Chapter 32

THEY WERE SAT AROUND the boss's comfortable living room. Three mismatched over-stuffed settees were placed in a group. Between them sat a massive wooden chest that served as a coffee table as well as storage. A fire roared in the grate.

Along one wall ran a series of period wall units made of oak panelling, but the wall units slid apart to reveal a state-of-the-art communications system. For now, the wall units remained tightly closed.

On the rug at Conrad's feet lay the latest member of the team – the stray dog who had travelled all the way from New Orleans to a small village in England and across time too.

"Did you bring the amulets with you?" asked the boss.

Toni immediately placed her artefact on the coffee table before them, then sat back in the soft cushions sipping her hot chocolate.

Conrad didn't move. He just stared into the fire.

"Conrad?" prompted the boss.

Conrad's attention snapped back as though he'd been daydreaming and was somewhere else, very far away. "What?" he said.

The boss moved his eyebrows and indicated the coffee table with his head. Conrad's eyes flicked from the boss to the table to Toni's amulet to Bart, who mimicked what the boss had done with his head. Reluctantly, Conrad reached into his pocket, pulled out a wad of fabric and slowly unwrapped his prize. He glanced down at the pendant in his hand, then slowly put it on the table in front of them.

"Why did you try to match the two amulets?" asked the boss.

Conrad shrugged his shoulders. He'd had a few days to come up with his story but didn't want it to sound too rehearsed. "I thought we needed the money."

"How would merging the two amulets bring us more money?"

"Placing them together and engaging them brings great wealth to the person doing it."

"And you had no intention of gaining that great wealth for yourself?"

"Of course not, little brother. What do you take me for?"

"I take you for someone who's been jealous of me inheriting the company and who has been trying to undermine me ever since."

"Come now, that's not very fair. You were complaining only the other week that you weren't sure we could afford to keep going for much longer."

Toni and Bart exchanged an uncomfortable look. This news was news to them.

The boss flicked a glance in their direction, but returned his attention to his brother.

"That was just me voicing a concern," he said. "I didn't expect you to go off into history to resolve it, putting Toni and Bart's lives at risk while you were at it."

"Their lives were never at risk," scoffed Conrad. "I was there waiting for them."

Without any proof, the boss couldn't really argue with his brother on that one. So he changed the subject. "What's this you've fetched home with you?" he said, indicating the dog.

"This is Sabot," said Conrad. The dog lifted his head at the sound of his name and Conrad gave him a scratch.

"Sabot?" said Bart.

"It means tramp in French," said Conrad. "He was a stray in New Orleans and he stowed away in the Model T Ford."

"I think he's lovely," said Toni, making kissing noises at the dog, who thumped his tail then lay back down again on the rug.

"He's my new partner," grinned Conrad. "He'll keep me company on future missions, give me someone to talk to."

The boss seemed to accept that and turned his attention to the two amulets. "We can't merge them," he reminded them all.

"Why not?" asked Conrad.

"Because they're not ours to merge. They're ours to keep safe and out of the wrong hands."

"But we don't have any money."

"We have plenty of money," smiled the boss.

"Where did we get it from?" asked Conrad.

"From a Miss Halima Dominique."

Silence crashed into the room like a deafening noise, and the three explorers looked at each other very puzzled.

"Miss Dominique?" asked Bart, perplexed.

"Yes. It's a long story."

"What happened?"

"In 1926, she was arrested at the Mardi Gras for using violent and threatening behaviour. But when they got her into custody, a friend who had accompanied her–"

"Koofrey Carbonneau?" interrupted Bart, sitting forward onto the edge of his seat.

"Yes," said the boss. "Or Koof as he preferred to be known. He convinced the sheriff's deputies to have a psychiatric evaluation done, which was unusual in those days. But it seems that Bart here convinced him to give it a try."

Bart had the good grace to blush.

"They decided that she was schizophrenic, when in fact she was just an alcoholic and a drug addict. But she was locked up in a sanatorium in the town for many, many years. Away from the temptation of absinthe and laudanum, she was soon in a lower security hospital that hadn't been built yet in 1926."

"But it had been built by 1948?" asked Toni. "The date we were supposed to go back to?"

"That's it. She became a volunteer nurse in the hospital first, then they gave her a job. And all the time her friend Koof was there by her side, keeping her on the straight and narrow, reminding her of the advice the English stranger had given him back in 1926."

"But the amulets?" said Conrad.

"She'd already joined them. She earned good money on the showboat and put it into a bank account in New Orleans that Koof opened for her, where it stayed until her eventual release from hospital."

"So are they useless now?" asked Toni.

"No. Because their power has already been used to bring great wealth to the person who merges them, to merge them again will undo all of that. There might be a financial crash or someone hacks into their account or for some reason their revenue is simply drained."

"What does it have to do with us?" asked Bart.

"When Koof searched you, Bart, you had a business card on you..." Bart thought for a moment, and then he remembered. "Koof and Miss Dominique were so happy with how her life turned out in the end, compared to how it could have done, that they sought us out."

"When did she die?" asked Toni.

"In the 1970s. She was very old."

"But you and Conrad were still boys then..."

"I know. But our father had already founded the organisation. Miss Dominique hired a private detective and, after a few long months, he came up with our father's company. And when she died, she left the surplus – after giving much to her own family – to the company. And, when Koof died too, not long after her in fact, he did the same. But the money didn't register until the moment in time that you helped her to get arrested, Bart."

"I don't understand," said Conrad.

"What don't you understand?" asked the boss.

"Why only a week or so ago the company was struggling and now, because of Bart, it isn't."

"Well, the money was there, but it started to disappear. I thought it was being syphoned off by a hacker or a fraudster. But when I looked into it, it's because someone went back to 1926 and started to meddle with history. Gradually, the money started to fade and our credit score was going through the floor. Nobody wanted to do new business with us, no one wanted to hire us to go back in time to maintain the balance. We were losing credibility, losing work and losing future revenue.

"It took me a while to work it out, but I knew that if someone had gone back to 1926 to collect the other amulet, all they had to do was find the one that would come to us anyway, put them together and undo the good that Miss Dominique had already done. I also picked up a vibe that they were going to try and stop her getting arrested and so stop the process that way."

"But I didn't go back until you said you were in trouble," said Conrad. This really was making his head hurt.

"I know," said the boss. "I think there may be someone else out there wanting to sabotage us. I thought it might be you at first, Conrad–"

"Me?!" Conrad was affronted.

"I know, and I'm sorry. But there must be someone else. And we need to find out who it is before they catch on and try to ruin us again."

"It's a bit scary really," said Bart. "That someone can do that and potentially change everything that we stand for."

"We obviously have some homework to do," agreed Toni. "How can we help?"

"Well," said the boss, stroking his chin. "First of all we need to get those two amulets placed into safekeeping as far enough apart as we can. We'll take the rest from there, but you might be off on another mission before too long."

"Great," said Conrad, ruffling his dog around the neck. "Me and Sabot here can get to know each other even better."

"Right then," said the boss, leaning forward. "Here are your next missions."

THE END

About the author

DIANE WORDSWORTH WAS born and bred in Solihull in the West Midlands when it was still Warwickshire. She started to write for magazines in 1985 and became a full-time freelance photojournalist in 1996. In 1998 she became sub-editor for several education trade magazines and started to edit classroom resources, textbooks and non-fiction books.

In 2004 Diane moved from the Midlands to South Yorkshire where she edited an in-house magazine for an international steel company for six years. She still edits and writes on a freelance basis.

Catch up with Diane today

Website: www.dianewordsworth.com
Facebook page: www.facebook.com/DMWordsworth/
Twitter: https://twitter.com/DMWordsworth
LinkedIn: www.linkedin.com/in/dianewordsworth

Also by Diane Wordsworth

Marcie Craig mysteries
Night Crawler: a Marcie Craig Mystery
Toni & Bart time-travel tales
Mardi Gras: a Toni & Bart time-travel tale
Short story collections
Twee Tales
Twee Tales Too
Twee Tales Twee
Writers' guides
Diary of a Scaredy Cat
Other non-fiction
A History of Cadbury
The Life of Richard Cadbury
Magazine
Words Worth Reading

Did you love *Mardi Gras*? Then you should read *Twee Tales*[1] by Diane Wordsworth!

A collection of twelve short stories by Diane Wordsworth, three of which are totally brand new. The other nine have all been previously published in UK magazines or broadcast on BBC local radio.

This book was previously published as *Twee Tales* by Diane Parkin Read more at https://dianewordsworth.com.

---

1. https://books2read.com/u/4DE07k

2. https://books2read.com/u/4DE07k

About the Author

Diane Wordsworth was born and bred in Solihull in the West Midlands when it was still Warwickshire. She started to write for magazines in 1985 and became a full-time freelance photojournalist in 1996. In 1998 she became sub-editor for several education trade magazines and started to edit classroom resources, textbooks and non-fiction books.

In 2004 Diane moved from the Midlands to South Yorkshire where she edited an in-house magazine for an international steel company for six years. She still edits and writes on a freelance basis.

Read more at https://dianewordsworth.com.